"Being a soldier was the only thing I ever wanted to do."

"Why?" She had to know why Hawk had chosen to be a ranger. "Why do you guys feel so committed to the army?"

"Because I fight for what I believe in. I love this country. I want to do my part." Not defensive, just powerful. Poignant. "Although it comes at a cost. I'm still single."

"Why haven't you gotten married?"

"Why get involved with someone when I knew I had to leave?"

"And yet being alone is the reason you stayed in the army?"

"It's a circular argument. Don't think I don't know that." He shrugged a shoulder, as if dismissing it, but something that looked like sadness clung to his features. "You're alone too, September. I don't have to ask to know the answer. You aren't dating."

"No. I don't have the heart left." She couldn't give voice to the loneliness of the past two years and the fear that she had been broken beyond repair. Beyond hope. Beyond God.

"We are two of a kind."

JILLIAN HART

grew up on her family's homestead, where she helped raise cattle, rode horses and scribbled stories in her spare time. After earning her English degree from Whitman College, she worked in travel and advertising before selling her first novel. When Jillian isn't working on her next story, she can be found puttering in her rose garden, curled up with a good book or spending quiet evenings at home with her family.

New York Times Bestselling Author

JILLIAN HART

THE SOLDIER'S HOLIDAY VOW

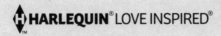
HARLEQUIN® LOVE INSPIRED®

Recycling programs
for this product may
not exist in your area.

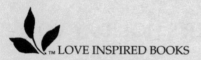

™ LOVE INSPIRED BOOKS

ISBN-13: 978-0-373-78865-1

The Soldier's Holiday Vow

www.Harlequin.com

Printed in U.S.A.

So let us come boldly to the throne of our gracious God. There we will receive his mercy, and we will find grace to help us when we need it most.
—*Hebrews* 4:16

Chapter One

September Stevens fought despair. Not an easy thing to do. The cold damp earth surrounded her like a grave. The jagged, crumbling walls of the mine shaft lifted above her and drank up the faint starlight. She and little Crystal Toppins had been down here for a good twelve hours. Sunset came early, near to four-thirty this time of year. That meant enough time had passed for it to be nearly midnight. If the sky wasn't partly overcast, typical for the Pacific Northwest in winter, the rising moon might have offered some relief from the suffocating dark and fear.

Maybe then it would have been easier to hold on to hope.

"They aren't coming, are they?" The ten-year-old girl gulped down a sob. It was too dark in the belly of the shaft to see more than a shadow of the child lying on her back on the earthen floor. Terror made the girl's voice thin and raw. "Are we going to d-die?"

"No, of course not." September leaned back against the hard-packed dirt wall and stretched her legs out as far as they would go. She had to believe that was the truth, but privately, she wasn't so sure. Crystal had been seriously hurt. September's injuries weren't as severe, but her left forearm had a compound fracture. With no antiseptic wipes, no sterile bandages and no first-aid kit—all of which were still packed safely in her saddle pack on her horse—she had done all she could.

She couldn't let her fear win. The horses would have returned to the stable, although it was miles away down Bear Mountain. Comanche was well trained and fond of his molasses snacks. He would have gone straight home and that meant Colleen, her boss, knew they were missing. Search parties would have gone out immediately—probably ten hours ago or so.

"They know where we were headed, so everyone knows where to look," she reasoned, putting as much reassurance as she could in her voice. Crystal's condition could be fragile, and she had to give the girl strength. "They are coming. They will be here as soon as they can."

"What if they can't find us? What if they stop looking?"

"They won't do that, sweetie." September pressed her arm against the girl's gently, comfortingly. "Do you think your mom would let that happen?"

"No." Crystal had to almost be smiling. "Mom's a little intense."

"Yes, she is, and that's a great thing. A fantastic thing. She will mow this mountain down to find you. I'm absolutely sure about that, so no more worrying. Got it?"

"Got it." Crystal sighed, a desolate sound in the dark.

A nearly absolute dark. September looked up through the ragged hole in the earth above to the disappearing stars. A cloud layer was moving in from the coast, blotting out the twinkling lights one by one. The dank chill of the ground crept into her bones, and it was a cold that gripped with talons. She would never be warm again.

Where was their search party? It was the question she had been asking since their horses balked, probably feeling the earth shift beneath their hooves. It was a good hour's ride back to the stable. That meant a search party should have been passing by within an hour, maybe two. Although she had listened diligently and watched carefully, there had been no sign of anyone riding the trail hunting for them. Did that mean no one would be coming? How long could they last, injured and without food or water or even a blanket for warmth? Was it possible they would die in this thirty-foot grave?

If so, this wasn't how she wanted to go, afraid and wishing she could change so much of her life. Her mess of a life. She drew in a rattling breath, leaned back against the cold earthen wall and closed her eyes against the thrum of pain inside her head. No one twenty-three years old should die with regrets. It wasn't right that she had so many of them.

If she had one do-over, it would be to go back in time exactly two years, two months and ten days and force Tim out of the army. To have made her fiancé realize that he had done his part in serving several tours of duty overseas. That he didn't have to stay in the military.

If she had been adamant, if she had stood her ground, then he would still be alive today and she wouldn't be in this abandoned shaft with an injured child weakening by the hour, bits of earth crumbling down on top of them.

Please, Lord. Send somebody before it's too late for Crystal. She sent the prayer heavenward, but feared it was not strong enough to escape this dark hole. Her faith was not exactly rock solid these days. She feared God had given up on her. She didn't blame Him one bit.

"I'm c-cold."

"Here, lean closer to me." She lifted her arm, carefully scooching closer to the injured girl. It was all she could offer.

The little girl leaned against her with another sigh, and September held her. She felt the fine chills of Crystal's body and feared she was slipping into shock. She could do nothing more for the child, who she feared was bleeding internally. Before the sun had gone down, there had been just enough light to see the growing bruise on the girl's abdomen. There was only so much basic first aid could do.

"September?" Crystal's voice sounded feeble, as if she were fading away. "What is it like to die?"

"I don't know." She felt the strike of the past, as if she was being pulled back to the cold, lifeless shock two years, two months and ten days ago. She had just turned into her driveway after coming home from the grocery store and seen the army chaplain and Tim's commanding officer at her front door.

She shut off her feelings to block the pain. After all this time, she still battled the overwhelming wave of grief. What had death been like for Tim? Had he known it was coming or was it so sudden, he didn't know? Had he suffered? Was his last thought of her? She hated how time had begun to dim his memory. She could no longer pull his image up in her mind as clearly. It felt doubly cruel.

"Jesus is supposed to be in heaven waiting for us, but what if I don't go there?" Crystal's voice wobbled. "What if I'm not good enough?"

"Jesus loves you, Crystal." She didn't feel equipped to be reassuring anyone's faith. "Please stop worrying and relax. You need to rest."

"Okay." The girl sounded all wrong—as if her condition were worsening, as if she were fading away.

Please, Lord, don't let that happen. It wasn't fair that Crystal had been so wounded when she had not been. She adjusted her broken arm carefully, where it rested on her thigh, and ignored the searing pain. *Take anything from me, Lord, and give it to Crystal. Please use it to save her life.*

No answer came. The last stars winked out. The little girl beside her gave a sob, as if she were running out of hope, too. September's stomach clamped tight with prickly fear for the girl. The truth was, she felt as if God could not see them and suspected He didn't care.

And wasn't that a sad way to feel? Her breath hitched in her lungs with a sharp pain. What happened to the woman she used to be? She dug deep, past the hard, suffocating shell of grief, and tried to see her old self, the one she had lost along with Tim and their dreams. *That* September would not be on the edge of despair. She would be certain God would see her to safety.

She'd had such perfect faith back then and doubt would never have crept in. Nor the certainty that she was forgotten in this grave deep in the earth.

How had she come to this place in her spiritual life? She felt blood trickling down her forehead—the cut must have started bleeding again—and gingerly blotted it with her T-shirt hem. The two years were a blur as she'd fought to put one foot in front of the other and make it through each minute, each hour, each day. Now she found herself here, trapped in the earth, more lost than she knew how to say.

"I feel real bad, September." Crystal sobbed once, just once.

"Hang in there, sweetie." She adored her little riding student; she felt useless to help her now. She tightened her hold on the girl. "Close your eyes and rest."

A snapping branch shattered the vast silence. Hope flared to life. She eased her arm around the girl and sat up, not daring to say anything or to even think the words. After all, it could be a wild animal passing by and not a rescue party. But still, it *could* be. She carefully rose upward, laying her good hand on the damp clay wall for support. Bright spots flashed in front of her eyes and the pounding in her head felt like the worst of thunderstorms. She kept her thoughts clear and strained for the tiniest sign that anyone was nearby.

"Hi, there." A man's rough baritone preceded the shine of a halogen flashlight.

There was something about that voice, both familiar and startling. Her thumping brain couldn't make sense of it right off. He took a moment to look away, as if signaling to more people out of her sight. Her double vision made it hard at first to recognize the striking, chiseled lines of his face, the high, proud forehead and straight bridge of his nose.

"You two are a welcome sight." He grinned down at her with an easy friendliness that spun her back in time.

"Hawk." Tim's best friend. Her blood went cold. Seeing his shadowed face sent her into another shock wave. Tremors quaked through her as she stared, openmouthed. The last time she'd seen him it had been dark, too, as dark as this mine shaft, the night full of loss and sorrow where no light could reach.

Why did it have to be him? Couldn't their rescuer be someone—anyone—other than Mark Hawkins?

"September Stevens, you look worse for the wear. Contusion. Concussion, maybe? Your arm's broken?"

She nodded, struggling to think past her shock. "Crystal's hurt. I think she needs a helicopter."

"Got it." Their gazes met and the force of it was like a punch. She knew without asking that he understood what she couldn't say, not without panicking the girl. He turned toward the child. "Crystal, hello there. Can you see me?"

"Ye-ah." She sounded weak. Too weak.

"Good, 'cause I'm comin' down to fetch you. You are the prettiest girl I've ever rescued." Unruffled, that was Hawk, and beyond the tough-as-bedrock Army Ranger was the heart of a truly kind man. He climbed into a harness and tied off. "Everything's gonna be fine now. You hear me?"

"Ye-ah." Even in terrible pain, the girl managed a small, brief smile.

September's knees were watery, so she sank back down beside the girl, watching as Hawk tested the rope and nodded to the other rescuers somewhere out of her sight. Good to go, he rappelled through the darkness, the rasp of the rope the only sound between them. Their ordeal was over, and they were found. That ought to bring her sheer relief. It didn't. Knowing their rescue came at the price of seeing Hawk again was no comfort. She winced when his feet hit ground. His presence seemed to draw every particle of air from the underground cave.

"We'll get Crystal up first," he murmured, leaning close. She could feel the heat radiating off his skin and smell the mix of mountain air, leather and exhaust clinging to his clothes. "We've got a chopper coming..." He paused to catch the gurney being lowered on a rope. "And Crystal's mom knows she's been found."

"Good." What a relief. She thought of Patty Toppins, a concerned, caring mom who had to be frantic with terror. Dully, she realized Hawk was kneeling next to Crystal. She cleared her throat. "Let me help."

"No need." His gloved hand caught hers and sent a shock through her system.

Alarmed, she wrenched her hand away, bumping into the earthen barrier. Her breathing came raggedly, her pulse thudded too loudly in her ears. Why had she reacted so strongly to Hawk's touch? Why had he unsettled her? She blinked, realizing another man was circling around to assist Hawk. Someone else roped down without her noticing. Too much was happening, and she couldn't seem to focus. It must be because of the concussion.

Hawk had already turned back to business, the wide set of his shoulders visible in the eerie shaft of light from above. It was good to see him. It was horrible to see him. She felt useless as the men started an IV for the girl and strapped her into the gurney. The second man hooked in. She caught a glimpse of Crystal's face, ashen in the harsh lighting, before the ground team hoisted her swiftly upward into waiting hands. The *whop-whop* of a helicopter told her help had arrived just in time.

"Let me take a look at you, September." Hawk's voice, gentle with concern. "You're hurt."

"Nothing like Crystal." It was too hard to look him in the eye, tougher still to see the shadows of the life and the dreams, which were gone. He reminded her of what was lost. Of the determined, competitive, patriotic man she had wanted to marry. A part of her had died right along with Tim. She wished she could step farther away from him, but there wasn't room enough to escape him. Stuck against the earth with nowhere to go, she was forced to stand while he inched closer. The cold damp seeped through her shirt and she shivered.

"Look up." Hawk shone a light into her eyes and flicked it away. He did it a second time, frowning.

She wanted to pretend he was a stranger, a man she did not know. It felt as if parts of her cracked again after she'd worked so hard to keep together. Panic crept through her and she pushed away. "I'm fine, Hawk. I just need to get out of here, that's all."

"I don't think you're fine. You're going to need stitches." His gaze raked across her face like a touch. "You've got quite a concussion. And what about that arm? That's going to need surgery."

"I'm alive. That's fine in my book." Maybe she sounded a little harsh, but it had been a terrible day and a worse night. Seeing him suddenly like this was the last thing she could deal with. She couldn't risk going back to that dark, broken place. "All I need is one of those harness things. Can you call up for one?"

"Better yet, you can ride with me." He sounded calm and unwavering. He was a fine soldier; seeing her again and remembering what had happened to Tim wasn't likely to throw him.

Unlike her. She caught sight of the extra harness hooked into his, and her knees wobbled. His hand shot out, steadying her by the elbow, the strength and heat of his touch seared like a burn. She didn't want to go up with him. "Maybe someone else—"

"We have to hurry, September." His gaze turned grim, the only hint at what he might be feeling. His shadowed face became a hard mask, impossible to read. "We don't want to keep the bird waiting."

"I don't need the helicopter."

"It's the best way." He had been calm on the night after they had buried Tim, too, a steady rock in the darkness. "I don't call the shots."

"But I don't want—" She couldn't finish. Her skull felt ready to explode from pain. Her stomach cramped with light nausea. She couldn't keep arguing with him, but how could she let him take her into his arms? She fisted her hands. She was not strong enough.

"You don't want to cost Crystal valuable time." Gentleness blended with cold-hard steel. He wrapped the harness around her hips and secured the strap, so close she could see the whorl of dark hair at his crown and smell the clean scent of his shampoo. His gaze latched on to hers with the force of the earth on the moon. "Put your arms around me."

If Crystal hadn't been waiting on her, she never would have done it. One thought of the girl had her wrapping her arms around Hawk's wide, muscled chest. She laid her cheek against his shirt pocket and squeezed her eyes shut, remembering the night she had refused his sympathy and the kind embrace of Tim's best friend.

His heart walloped beneath her ear. The fabric of his BDUs roughly caressed her cheek as the iron band of his arms embraced her. The rope tugged, lifting them off the ground.

She had to will away the memories whispering at the edges of her mind and force them into silence again. Looking back wouldn't change the truth. It wouldn't make her whole and strong again. It wouldn't return Tim to her. Would Hawk understand that? They began to sway, oddly buoyant as the rope drew them upward.

"You doin' okay?"

She nodded.

"You're not gonna pass out on me, are you?"

Choosing silence again, she shook her head. Hands were reaching out for her.

"Careful of her left arm," Hawk called out.

She felt someone grab her good arm to hoist her to her feet. She opened her eyes to see the gloomy bowl of the sky and the brightly lit wooded area. A dozen search-and-rescue team members were busy at work, manning the ropes, running the lights or talking on squawking radios. A search dog barked at his handler, excited by her arrival, as if he had been worried, too. She looked everywhere but at the man with one arm still around her. Even on solid ground, she felt as if she were swaying in midair.

Hawk was talking, rattling off her injuries, unhooking the carabineer connecting them, and her harness fell away. Other soldiers helped her onto a gurney. She didn't want to, but her head was spinning. She realized the volunteers were from nearby Fort Lewis, where the Ranger battalion Tim had belonged to was stationed. She'd been introduced to some of the men at one time or another, men who were faceless now in the shadowy dark. She let them strap her down and check her vitals.

"You did great." He knelt at her side, his hair slick with sweat, and his granite face compassionate. "You saved that girl's life. You knew what to do and you did it."

"I didn't do much. I raised her feet. I kept her quiet. I gave her my sweatshirt."

"It's the simple stuff that can make the most difference. You kept her as stable as you could until help came." The gurney bounced as the men lifted her. He stayed by her, carrying his share of her weight. "You did good."

"I know what you're doing. You're distracting me from my injuries so they don't seem as bad."

"Someone will splint that arm for you in the

chopper. I'm glad you're okay, September. I'm glad I found you." He kept his voice casual and easy.

"Thank you, Hawk."

"Sure thing." He kept his footing, not easy on the rocky edge of the steep trail. They were closer to the bird now, the engine noise making it too loud to say much. He had enough light to see her better, the silk of her cinnamon-brown hair, her smooth creamy complexion and her lovely, oval face. She was not the same woman he remembered. Gone was her sparkle, her quick, easy manner that twinkled like summer stars. Sure enough, Tim's loss had been hard on her.

She wasn't alone with that.

Strange how God worked, he thought, as he ducked against the draft from the blades. While he hadn't seen her in years, time and the rigors of active duty hadn't obliterated her from his memory.

Why was it so easy to remember the good times? They flashed through his mind unbidden and unwanted. Seeing her picture for the first time when Tim had dug it out of his wallet after joining their battalion. Meeting her at a bowling party when their scheduled picnic had been rained out—typical Seattle-Tacoma weather. Hearing about her in the letters Tim read when they'd been sharing a tent and griping good-naturedly about their time in the desert. Those were innocent times, before he'd lost one of his lifelong friends. Before he'd had to deal with the harsh realities of war.

"On three," their sergeant barked, and they lifted her into the chopper. Hawk hopped in after, glancing at Crystal, stabilized and prepped, before his gaze lingered on September's face. Even in the harsh light, she was beautiful.

"You want me to call anyone?" he asked her, taking her good hand, careful of the IV. "Your mom?"

"Don't trouble her. I can take care of myself." That was it, no more explanation. She didn't meet his gaze.

He could feel the wall she put up between them like a concrete barrier. Was she mad because he had missed Tim's funeral? His plane had come in late. He'd flown halfway around the world, and military transports weren't the most on-time birds in the sky. Had she been alone? Tim's brother, Pierce, had been there, but he couldn't remember the details, like if her family lived nearby. Anyway, he and Pierce had flown out that night, leaving her desolated in the cold rain.

"Anyone else I can contact?"

"There's no one." She turned her head away and swallowed hard, as if she were in emotional pain. The shadows hid her, but he could feel her sadness.

The captain tapped him on the shoulder. Time to go. He hated that he couldn't say goodbye; she didn't want to hear it. He hated what his presence was doing to her. Some memories were best left buried. He knew how that was.

His boots hit the ground, and he got clear. Dirt rose up in clouds as the bird took off, hovering off the ground for a moment as if battling gravity, then turning tail and lifting purposefully into the starless black.

"Was that September Stevens, Tim's former fiancée?" Reno asked as they watched the taillights grow distant.

"Yep." That was all he could say. Something sat in his throat, refusing to let him say more. He, Tim and Pierce had all been buddies since they were kids. They'd been neighbors back home in Wyoming, running wild in the foothills of the Rockies. They'd called themselves the dynamic trio back then, naive kids in a different world. War had changed that. War changed a lot of things.

He thought of September and her broken heart. There was some serious pain there. He felt for her, but it was why he kept clear of relationships. His life as a Ranger wasn't conducive to long-term commitment. It was his experience that love didn't necessarily grow fonder half a world apart. What he did was dangerous. Tim hadn't been the only soldier buried over the recent conflicts defending this country's freedom. He couldn't justify putting a woman through that, waiting and wondering, fearing with every phone call or knock on the door that he was dead. Seeing September was all the proof he ever needed of that.

He couldn't say why, but she stayed on his mind, a sad and beautiful image he could not forget.

Chapter Two

"How are you feeling today?" The hospital volunteer flashed a sunny smile as she set the bouquet of flowers onto September's bedside table.

"Better." In some ways, but not in others. She smoothed the wrinkles out of her hospital gown. For one thing, this had to go. She felt vulnerable in it. She carefully adjusted her casted forearm on the pillow. "I get to go home."

"Great news." The volunteer stepped back to admire the small collection of flowers. "I'm going to come by the riding stable you work for. I've always wanted to take lessons. I don't suppose you teach beginners. I don't even have a horse."

"You can rent one along with your lesson. It's done all the time." September reached for the pen and notepad on the bedside table, ignored the twinge of pain in her skull and the bite beneath her cast. She scribbled down the stable's phone number. "When you call, ask for me. I'll give your first lesson free, although you will have to spring for the horse rental."

"That would be fantastic. Thank you." The volunteer brightened and looked younger than September had first guessed. Maybe in her early thirties or late twenties. It reminded her that everyone went through tough times. Everyone had a challenging road to walk. The volunteer padded to the door. "Oh, it looks like you have a visitor. A *totally* handsome one."

That could only mean one man—Hawk. She didn't know anyone else who could be described as *totally* handsome. She expected dread to build inside her like a river dam, but it didn't.

"Hey there." Hawk waited for the volunteer to clear the room before he leaned one brawny shoulder against the doorjamb. He clutched a small vase of gardenias in one capable hand. "Thought I would swing by and check on you. See how you're doing."

"Good, considering." She hugged the bedcovers to her, aware that they were practically alone together. The nurses at the station a few doors down felt very far away.

"You look much better than the last time I saw you. Trust me." A hint of a grin tugged at the spare corners of his mouth, but his gaze remained serious and kind. "I hear they're springing you today."

"Yes, they're releasing me on my own recognizance." She wanted to keep things light and on the surface, to hide the fact that she was numb inside, like winter's frozen ground. It was better that way. This was how she had survived Tim's burial and moved on. Today was simply another day, like so many had been, one she needed to get through one step at a time, one breath, one moment. Seeing Hawk didn't change a thing.

"I meant to come by sooner, but you know how it is. Duty calls." He strode into the room like some kind of action hero, confident and athletically powerful and mild mannered all at once. "I didn't know if you wanted to see me again, but I had to look at you and know for myself that you are going to be all right."

It hurt to look at him. Not only because of Tim—but also because of the hardship etched on Hawk's face. She studied him as he set the vase on the night table with the several other arrangements, the sweet gardenia scent mixing pleasantly with the roses and carnation bouquets. Her skin prickled at his nearness like a warning buzzer going off to announce that he was too near. She could smell the sunshine on his T-shirt and the faint scent of motor oil on his faded denims.

This close, she could see the lines etched at the corners of his eyes, ones that hadn't been there the last time she'd seen him. She wrapped her arm around her middle like a shield. He'd had his losses, his trials and his sorrows. She was not looking at the same man she'd once known as Hawk, in those long-ago-seeming days before Tim's death. War and loss had changed him, too.

"You have family coming for you?" The sunlight from the window spilled over him, gilding him. With his muscled frame straight and strong, he resembled the noble warrior he was.

And exactly why was she noticing that? She had no interest in love anymore. She would never fall for another soldier. It was that simple. She stared hard at a fraying thread in the hem of the blanket covering her instead of meeting his gaze. "My sister is running late. She's taking me home."

"You still have an apartment near the post?"

"No." She was surprised he had remembered

her little one-bedroom place in a pretty gray building along a greenbelt. He'd attended Tim's birthday party, the only one Tim had been home for through their entire relationship. "I've got a town house now, not far from where I work."

He didn't say the obvious, that both she and Tim had been saving up to buy a house after they were married. She had invested her savings in a place of her own instead.

"Look, September. I never thought we'd meet again." He squared those impressive shoulders of his. "I thought about looking you up and seeing how you were. But I was afraid it would be too painful for you. I can see it is."

"It's okay." She wasn't the only one hurting. She might not have known him well—he'd been one of Tim's best friends, not hers—but she could see he had walked a hard road, too. "I've thought about finding you or Tim's brother, on and off. I wanted to, but I could never make myself do it."

"You wanted to see me?"

She nodded. He and Tim had been together at those last moments. Hawk held the answers to the questions that had kept her wondering. But would asking them bring up as much sadness for him as it did for her? "You missed his funeral."

"Not my idea, but I made it for the wake. I didn't get a chance to talk to you." His brows knit together and he leaned back against the wall, pensive and dark. "You could have asked me then, but you refused to speak to me."

"I was hurting too much. I wasn't ready to hear about what happened over there. I had lost my one true love. I was torn apart. I couldn't stand to know the details."

"Don't blame you there."

"But I had questions later. After the first shock of loss faded, I thought of all the things I should have asked, things that I needed to know. And you were far away and unreachable."

"I'm sorry about that." He felt helpless. He should have looked her up. He should have made sure she was all right.

"There's a part of me that doesn't want to know the answers." Her confession came as softly as a hymn, resonating deep within him.

Ranger School had taught him how to lead, how to fight and how to accomplish his goal the right way, no excuses allowed. He might have led missions in the most dangerous places in the world, but facing the pretty brunette in front of him, he was at a loss. He was well trained and fearless, but right now all his training meant little. He did not know how to ease her grief. She had loved Tim deeply.

"You let me know which side wins out." It was all he could do for her. "If you want answers, I will give you what I can."

"Thanks, Hawk, and the flowers are lovely. My favorite." Although she sat straight and sweetly, the corners of her mouth fought to hold steady. Shadows dimmed the bronze depths of her eyes, which had once sparkled and twinkled with abundant joy.

It was hard seeing the change in her. She looked like a woman who no longer laughed or who no longer knew how to live. Sympathy squeezed his hard heart. "I picked up a few things hanging out with the Granger brothers. Tim was always sending you gardenias. I figured there had to be a reason."

"A slight one." She didn't need to say how much she had appreciated that about her man.

Hawk could see it. He felt drawn to her in a way that was beyond sympathy. The tightness in his chest was much more than a man's concern over a woman he had rescued. The past connected them like a bridge across a river, taut and undeniable. He'd been a fool to come; it had been the right thing, but foolish. In the end, he couldn't stay away. "I made a mistake with the flowers. They've reminded you of Tim."

"Yes, but it was thoughtful." She tried to put a bandage on her pain with a tentative smile, but he wasn't fooled.

"I didn't think. I just remembered—"

"I know," she interrupted, saving him from feeling in the wrong. She was gentle and kind that way. Lovely, not just on the outside but inside, where it truly counted. "I haven't received flowers in a long time. Now look at all of this. Fall down an old mine shaft and I get all this attention."

She was trying to steer away from talk of the past and of everything that hurt, too. Relieved, he went with it and put on a grin. Maybe it was best to leave sad things in the shadows. "How did you get down there, anyway?"

"You don't want to know." She played with the blanket hem, her long, sensitive fingers working a blue thread. Her sleek brown hair fell around her face like a shield. "I made a mistake."

"Who hasn't at one time or another?"

"I should have been more strict with Crystal, but she's one of my favorite students."

"Plus, you are a pushover. At least, that's my best impression of you."

"I've been called worse." She twirled a loose thread around her fingers, hating the way her hand trembled. She fought to stay numb, keeping the broken pieces safely frozen as if they were nothing, nothing at all. "Crystal's mare was sidestepping and acting weird."

"In my opinion, horses always act weird."

"That's because they aren't always predictable. Even the best-trained horse will surprise a good rider."

"Even you?" He arched one dark brow. "I've heard you are quite the horsewoman."

"Believe me, I know plenty who are better riders than I will ever be. Especially when Crystal refused to get back on the trail. When her horse balked, I should have insisted she dismount immediately. I already had, and I was reaching for her mare's bridle."

"You must have trouble with wildlife on that mountainside."

"Yes, and if a horse sees a predator, there's no guarantee you can hold them. Crystal is a strong-minded girl, I adore her, but she was testing my patience by not listening. Then the ground gave out. Her mare must have sensed the earth wasn't steady. She took off, threw Crystal. I hit a back hoof on the way down. We fell a long way. My horse had already taken a few steps off the trail and had calmed down."

"Both horses wound up back home okay."

"Yes, and I'm grateful. Comanche is a good boy. He's the reason you found us."

"Yes. It's the reason we knew where to start looking. At first they thought Crystal's dad might have abducted her. That threw everyone off for a bit."

"Oh." She hadn't considered that. She knew a little of her students' private lives, but not too much. She was aware the family had been through a bitter divorce. "I can't imagine how terrified Patty must have been."

"We were called in around chow time to help with the search." Hawk pushed away from the wall and grabbed a hard-backed chair by the top. He swung it toward the bed, seating himself on it like a motorcycle.

"I should have realized they would have called over to Fort Lewis for help with search and rescue."

"Then, what, you would have been better prepared to see me?" Kindness warmed his intense blue gaze. "You couldn't have known I would be on post at all. Just like I couldn't have known when I took a look at who we were searching for that they would hand me your picture."

"No." She swallowed hard, as if not pleased they had circled back around to the past, which was an impossible river between them.

"It's going to be all right, September." He reached out, his warm callused hand settling on her forearm. "We don't have to talk or think about it. We'll chalk it up to divine providence and go on from here."

"Good plan." She tried to think straight, but the sunlight blazed strangely bright until she could not see. Maybe it had something to do with her concussion. When the sun faded to its usual midmorning glow, Hawk gazed with concern at her, appearing as solid and as unyielding as a granite mountain. She swallowed hard, trying to act normal. "You must be up for deployment soon."

"I'll be Stateside for a while, but you know that can change at a drop of a hat."

"I do. You've been a Ranger for a long time. You like the lifestyle."

"Seven years." He shook his head, scattering

what there was of his short dark hair. "You're doing well for yourself. I hear you have a reputation at what you do."

"A good one, I hope."

"Very good, from what everyone at the stables told me. You've done an admirable job, September. I wish I could say I've got my life together the way you have yours."

"Why do you say that? I thought you loved your job."

"Now, I never said that exactly. I love being a Ranger, but it comes at a high cost. I almost opted out. Losing my best friend was hard on me. In the end I feel committed to what I do. I don't think I will ever give up the military. Although you have a nice peaceful life here. Spending your days doing what you love. It's got to be a good gig."

"I like it." She tried to resist the pull of his kindness. "It's not saving the world."

"There are many ways to save the world. Teaching kids to ride and show their horses, that's a good way for them to spend their time. Instead of some alternatives."

"I've never thought of it that way. There are a lot of good life lessons in caring for a horse and establishing a trusting relationship."

"Maybe that's where I went wrong in life. I didn't have a horse." He winked at her, but she got the feeling he was covering up something that saddened him. He rose from the chair and swung it back into its original place. "Well, I don't want to take up more of your time. I'm glad you're doing well, that's what I had to know."

"Thanks to you." Her throat tightened, and if she didn't say it now, then she never would. "It was easier seeing you again this time, when I expected it."

"You knew I would drop by?"

"Yes. It's something a man like you would do." She blushed at the compliment she paid him, feeling uncomfortable and vulnerable when she didn't want to feel anything at all. "When we were in the mine and I first saw your face, I knew everything was going to be all right."

"That has to do with you, September, the woman you are. I did my job, that's all."

How she wished she could turn back time and work it so her life and Tim's could have turned out differently. She would give anything to fix what had been broken, both in her and for

Hawk, as well. He'd lost one of his best friends, a friend he hadn't been able to protect.

She didn't know what to say to him as he crossed toward the door. A knock startled her. Her sister hurried into the room with a duffel bag slung over her shoulder and gave Hawk a narrow look.

"And here I thought you would be bored waiting for me." Chessie backtracked. "I didn't know you had a visitor. I can come back. I'm dying for a cup of tea."

A seed of panic took root between September's ribs. Panic, because her sister had jumped to the wrong conclusion—that she and Hawk were interested in each other. Even the thought of opening herself up like that again terrified her. "No, stay."

A little too abrupt, September, she told herself. Hawk had to have heard the sharpness in her tone. What was he thinking?

"No need." His rich, buttery baritone rang reassuringly. "I'm on my way out. September, you take care now."

"You, too, Hawk." The words squeaked out of her throat.

His gaze fastened on hers, making the room and her sister's presence fade away. She saw something akin to her own wounds shadowed there, hiding in his eyes. Her pulse skyrocketed over the fact that she wanted something she no longer believed in.

"I hope you find that happy ending you always wanted. You deserve it, September." His voice resonated with sincerity. Saying nothing more, he nodded in acknowledgment to her sister and strode from the room. The pad of his boots on the tile faded to silence, but his presence somehow remained.

"Good-looking guy." Chessie poked her head around the door frame to get another look. "Who is he?"

"One of the Rangers from Fort Lewis who found Crystal and me." She breathed a sigh of relief, troubled by the man and his shadows. At least he understood. He had his wounds, deeper and more severe than hers could ever have been. War could do that to a man.

"There was road construction. Sorry. I should have remembered, but you know me, too much on my mind." Chessie plopped the duffel on the foot of the bed and unzipped it. "So, are you going to date him?"

"Date Hawk?" There was a picture she couldn't quite bring into focus. "Hardly."

"I had to ask. You never know. Time heals all wounds. I know it doesn't seem like it now, but one day things will be better."

"I'm sure you're right." She didn't believe it, but she didn't want to drag her sister down. "Did you remember to bring shoes?"

"Are you kidding? There's nothing more important than shoes." Chessie pulled a pair of snazzy boots from the bottom of the bag. "Ta-da. See, your big sister won't ever let you down."

"You're one blessing I'm grateful for." She smiled, trying too hard to find the normalcy her life had once been. It didn't work, but she hoped she looked as if it did. She feared she would always feel out of sync, as if she were looking at her own life through a foggy mirror. She thought of Hawk and wondered what he was doing with his day off. She wondered how he managed to walk in the light with so many wounds in his soul.

Hawk strode through the automatic doors and into the blinding sunlight. The cool kiss of the mid-December breeze felt pleasant against his skin. He'd stopped by to see the little girl, Crystal, but she was in ICU and not taking any visitors. He'd met her mom, though, and learned that they expected to move her out onto a floor that afternoon. Things were looking up. He'd left a balloon bouquet with Patty, and that was that. He had no more reason to think about September Stevens. So, why was she on his mind?

It was a mystery. Loose ends, maybe, or just the fact that their paths had crossed. He hauled his bike key from his pocket, fiddling with it as he hiked toward the parking lot. If only he could have stayed away. Seeing her again tied him up in knots, and he was afraid to look at those tangled threads too closely.

He straddled his Harley and plugged in the key. While the engine rumbled, he hauled his helmet off the backrest and that's when he saw her. His gaze drew to her like fate. September, in a mandatory wheelchair, emerged from the automatic doors onto the concrete walkway, with his gardenias in her arms.

How pretty she looked. She wore a light pink T-shirt that said Ride for the Cure, jeans and black riding boots. Her softly bouncy hair shone like cinnamon in the sunshine. She was still as sweet as ever. She'd always been delicate and kind, and not even life's hardships had changed that. He surely hoped that God had been watching over her specially, as he'd kept her in prayer.

He would never forget seeing her after the funeral, an image of perfect grief. He'd been in awe of her. What would it be like to love so much? To have been loved like that?

He tugged on his helmet and yanked on the straps to secure them. Across the way, a light blue SUV crawled to a stop at the curb, and September's sister emerged from it. With a hurried gait, she started loading the flowers several hospital volunteers were carrying. They scolded September for standing and trying to help out. He spotted a few arrangements already in the back of the SUV.

He grabbed the grips and fed the engine. The bike gave a satisfying roar. Something kept him from leaving. Maybe it was the sight of September, pale and fragile with a bandage on her forehead and a pink cast on her left arm. Yep, that got to him. He couldn't hold back the pounding need to look after her. He wanted to be the one to take care of her. It wasn't a conscious choice. It simply came into being.

With one last look, he rolled the bike backward out of the parking space and released the clutch. The Harley shot forward, taking him away from September, but not from the thought of her.

Chapter Three

Chessie set the last vase of flowers in the middle of the breakfast bar and fussed with it, turning the vase to get it just right. "So, time to fess up. What's the deal?"

"About what?" September looked up from her position on the couch, sorting her mail. A surprising amount of junk had accumulated during the two days she'd been in the hospital.

"Not what. Who." Satisfied with the way the flowers looked, Chessie dropped into one of the bar chairs. "What was Mark Hawkins really doing in your hospital room?"

"The obvious. Bringing flowers. Seeing how I was."

"I didn't know you had anything to do with that life anymore."

She meant army life. September sighed, remembering the tough time her sister had given her over her decision to date a Ranger and then accept his marriage proposal. She tossed a handful of advertisements into the paper-recycling bin. "I haven't seen Hawk since the funeral."

"Talk about coincidences."

"You have no idea."

"Not a good coincidence."

"No." Her heart twisted hard, remembering how Hawk had changed. What had happened to him? "I'm trying to move on with my life, and it's not easy. Something always pops up to pull me back." Something forced her to remember when life had been bright and her dreams shiny and new.

"He should know that. He should have left you alone." Chessie, protective big sister, folded her arms across her chest. "Want me to talk to him?"

"No. He meant well. Besides, it's not like I'm going to see him again. As if. He will probably be TDY by the end of the week."

"You mean on a tour of duty?" Chessie relaxed and propped her chin on her fists. "All right, I won't hunt him down. But that doesn't mean you're okay. You didn't need a reminder of your losses."

"True." She tossed a few more envelopes thick with coupons she would never need. "He looks hardened. No longer the carefree guy I remember."

"War will do that, I suppose. It's his choice to do what he does, carrying a gun and shooting people with it." Chessie had a strong opinion on that. She had strong opinions on just about everything. "Don't worry, I will stay off my soapbox, but what kind of man does that year after year?"

The kind who cares about others more than himself. September kept quiet. She wasn't up to any kind of serious discussion about the rights and wrongs of war. Nor did she remind her sister that those words maligned Tim's memory. Tim who had died trying to save innocent embassy hostages. Hawk had been wounded on that mission, she remembered. The hows and whys were a mystery to her.

"I'm going to swing by and pick up some pizza. That ought to put a smile on your face." Chessie slid off the chair and hooked her purse strap over her shoulder. "I'll get a dessert pizza, too. The Stevens girls are going to totally carb out."

"Sounds just like what I need." Comfort food

all the way. She flung the last junk mail envelope into the bin. There, done with that chore. Not that there weren't a dozen more needing to be done around here. Clutter was accumulating. She needed to give her family room and kitchen area a serious going-over. Keeping busy would keep her mind off her troubles, right?

"What are you doing?" Chessie scolded from the doorway. "I see you getting up. You're going to do housework, aren't you?"

"Why do you say that like an accusation?" September swiped a stack of books off the coffee table and tucked them into the crook of her good arm. "I have pizza coupons you can use."

"I have some in my car." Chessie closed the door and crossed through the living room. "That's it, I'm calling for delivery. Someone needs to keep an eye on you. Now lie down. Do it now, or I'll make you."

"This sounds exactly like my childhood," she quipped, reluctantly putting down the books. "No one can understand the hardship I went through as your sister."

"Ha, ha." Chessie tapped her foot, pointing to the arm of the couch where she'd propped two fluffy down pillows earlier. "Feet up. I mean it—"

The doorbell rang. She was saved. She kept

her feet firmly on the hardwood floor. "Should I get that?"

"As if." Chessie huffed out a frustrated sigh as she pivoted on her Mary Janes and marched through the town house. "You stay right where you are, sister dear. You just got out of the hospital and you're going to take care of yourself even if I have to—"

She opened the door and fell silent. Curious, September leaned forward far enough on the cushions to see a uniformed delivery dude holding pizza boxes.

"Got a delivery for Hawkins," he announced.

"Hawkins?" That had her moving across the room. She was halfway to the door before she saw the black motorcycle pulling up to the curb out front. Hawk swung off his bike, unbuckling his helmet.

"I'll sign for it." He slung his helmet over the backrest while the delivery guy handed Chessie the pizzas. The look on her sister's face wasn't a good one.

What was Hawk up to now? Why was he here? She hadn't recovered from seeing him in the hospital. She hadn't recovered from seeing him at all. Why did he have to show up looking so alive and vital?

"What aren't you telling me?" Chessie asked as they watched Hawk sign the charge slip with an efficient scribble.

"Not one thing."

"I hope you're right. I'll take these to the kitchen." Chessie tapped away, her tone cool.

The sunlight graced him, but he was a man who walked as if he did not notice. He'd turned grim over the last hard years, and his strong, granite face, which had always been quick to grin, was serious.

She held the door for him, watching as he strode up the walkway. She couldn't stop from caring. Well, not the serious kind of caring. What she felt was sympathy, she told herself, understanding for the man who had rescued her. Nothing more complicated than that.

"Hope you don't mind." He slipped the receipt into his wallet. "I figured you wouldn't be up to cooking and your sister might appreciate a little help."

"It was nice of you." She didn't need to wonder if there was a deeper motive or a hidden agenda. He was a straightforward guy. She liked Hawk; she had always liked him, and why wouldn't she? He had been a good friend to Tim. He was a good man. That's what she would concentrate on and not the past, not the hurt. She pulled open the door a little wider in welcome. "Why don't you come in and have lunch with us?"

"I don't mean to impose. I wondered if there was anything I could do for you. Run some errands or something." He crossed the threshold, towering over her. "I'm good at fetching."

"Are you sure you don't have anything better to do?"

"Positive." His humble grin reassured her.

He was merely being kind, the way Tim would have wanted. That realization made her heart squeeze shut. There was the past, yawning wide open, full of everything she had lost. Best to pretend it wasn't there, a void between them. Dully, she let him take charge of the door and close it.

"I didn't know what kind of pizza you like," he explained, "so I got a couple different combos."

"It smells delicious. When it comes to pizza, I'm not picky. As long as it has a crust and cheese, I'm happy. Thanks, Hawk."

"No problem. I'm glad to see you doing better." He jammed his hands into his jean pockets, matching his stride to hers as they crossed through the living room. "You gave me a good scare when I first saw you in that mine."

"I was pretty scared myself." She ignored the look her sister gave her and reached up into the kitchen cabinets for three plates. "But it was only a few stitches."

"Don't forget the surgery. What do you think you're doing?" Hawk sidled in behind her and took the plates before she could lift them from the shelf. "Go sit down. I'm thinking your sister will agree with me."

"That's right," Chessie answered curtly from across the room.

"I'm fine." Sure, her arm hurt, but she wasn't about to be waited on. She could take care of herself.

"You had best stay off your feet, September. You need to heal." His warm, caring baritone wrapped around her like a wool blanket, soothing and tender. Caring was in the layers of his voice, in the lines crinkling pleasantly at the corners of his eyes, in the space between them.

He really is a nice man, she thought. She simply had to be careful so the memories couldn't hurt her. So he couldn't hurt her. She slipped away from the counter and from him. "Nobody needs to worry about me. It was a hard fall, true, but I wasn't hurt like Crystal. Did you hear? She's doing better. I heard from her mom that she was already asking when she could go riding again."

"That's a good sign. She's a trooper. I hope she's back in the saddle before long."

"Me, too. You were great with her. I know all about your training, of course, but to see it in action, it was impressive."

"Just your tax dollars at work." He opened the box tops for Chessie, so she didn't have to put down her plate to dish up, but his gaze remained firmly on September. "You kept the girl alive until help came. You made a real difference."

"I didn't do much, and you already said that earlier."

"That doesn't make it less true." He took the next plate, watching her carefully. "Ham and pineapple or the works?"

"A slice of both, please." She was ashen, all the color drained from her cheeks, her wide brown eyes too big for her face. Had his presence done that to her? Or her ordeal? She looked fragile with her casted arm in a sling.

"I'll dish you up. Go ahead and sit down," he told her. "Join your sister."

She nodded once in acknowledgment, watching him closely with appreciation or caution, he couldn't tell which. Maybe a little bit of both. He chose the largest slices and slid them onto her plate, aware of every step she took through the kitchen of granite counters and white cabinets to the seating arrangement in a sunny bay window nook. Her sister spoke to her in low tones, and the murmur of women's voices was a strange, musical sound he wasn't accustomed to. But he liked it. He was more used to the sound of plane engines, gunfire in the shooting range and barked orders rising above it all in a no-nonsense cadence.

He reached for the last plate and served himself two slices of the works. Why was he here? He couldn't quite say. He wanted to believe he'd come because Tim would have wanted him to make sure September was well.

That wasn't the whole of it. He had to be honest. He closed the tops to the pizza boxes and crossed over to the women. His boots knelled as loud as a jackhammer on her wood floor, or at least it felt that way because when the women looked up, their conversation silenced. One studied him with suspicion, the other with a hint of care. That surprised him. Her caring couldn't be personal. He'd never had the chance to know September much, it was hard to get to know any civilian with his job, but he knew she was gentle and kind to all she met—even to a guy like him. Emotion tugged within him, distant and unfamiliar, and he dismissed it. He was simply glad for the luxury of her company, that's all.

"The motorcycle is new," she began after her sister said the blessing. "I didn't know you rode."

"Since high school, but I sold my Honda after I enlisted." He tried not to look at her. Maybe it would make the unaccustomed feelings within him fade instead of live. "Last year I realized I missed riding, so I got another bike. I figured why not?"

Small talk. That's what this was. It was uncomfortable. Maybe he shouldn't have stayed, he thought, as he took his first bite of pizza. The taste of spicy sauce, cheese, dough and pepperoni ought to overpower everything he was feeling, but it didn't come close. He cared about her. He hadn't planned on it, but his feelings were there just the same. The threads knotted up inside him tightened; he didn't dare look at those hidden feelings.

"I had forgotten." She set her pizza on her

plate. The tiniest bite had been taken from the end of the slice. "You, Tim and his brother, Pierce, had dirt bikes when you were kids."

"My mom didn't like the idea of me speeding around on the back of a motorized bike, as I was prone to getting hurt on the regular two-wheeled variety, but I didn't relent and she finally gave in. Tim, Pierce and me, we rode far and wide. I think at one point we knew every trail and old forgotten logging road in two national forests."

"It sounds similar to how we grew up, right, Chessie?" September glanced across the table at her sister, and her look said, *Play nice.*

He appreciated that. The table was a small round one, and that meant there wasn't much room between him and either lady. He could feel icy dislike radiating off September's sister like vapor off dry ice. The only thing worse was the awareness of September, how she was close, how he wanted her to be closer. He wanted to comfort her. Even he could see that she'd hit a rough patch.

"Instead of dirt bikes, we had horses." When she spoke of times past, the shadows in her eyes softened. The corners of her mouth upturned with a hint of a smile.

"Those had to be good times," he found himself saying, as if to urge her on. As if he wanted to hear more.

"They were. We had the sweetest little mare to learn on. Clyde was twenty-two years old. Our dad was worried about us getting hurt—we were in grade school—so he would only let us get a very old and even-tempered horse."

"Sounds like he was a good dad."

"The best." Dad was the reason she'd grown up living her childhood dream. He and Mom had sacrificed a lot so she could have Comanche. "He wanted us to live our dreams and he did all he could to help us work for them. Right, Chessie?"

She looked to her sister, maybe to include her in the conversation and also for an unspoken need for sisterly support. He had the distinct feeling she was uncomfortable with him. She kept avoiding direct eye contact. Maybe dropping by hadn't been his smartest idea ever.

"Dad is stellar. They don't make men like him anymore." The older, sterner sister's tone implied that Hawk fell short. Very short.

"There are plenty of good men," September said gently. "Chessie and I were fortunate enough to take riding lessons. When we were older, we both worked in the barn to earn board for our show horses. We were suburb girls, but Mom drove us the twenty-three-mile trip each way twice a day. Sometimes more."

"Sounds like a good mom." His mom had suffered from depression after his dad's passing, which was why he'd practically grown up with the neighboring Granger boys. He would have explained it all to September, but that would mean bringing up a past she shouldn't have to deal with. Instead, he kept it simple and in the moment. "She obviously loved you both."

"And we love her. After the divorce, she remarried and moved to San Francisco. We don't see her like we used to, but she's happy." Longing weighed down her voice. Clearly she was close to her mother.

"My dad died when I was in third grade." The words were out before he could draw them back. Once said, they couldn't be unspoken. So much for his decision not to mention the past. He shrugged a shoulder, as if that past couldn't hurt him anymore. "She never got over it."

"Sometimes a woman doesn't." The shadows in her beautiful eyes deepened, like twilight falling.

The human heart was a fragile thing, capable of great, indestructible love and yet able to infinitely break. He bit into his second slice of pizza, crunching on a few green peppers, thinking. He didn't believe in coincidence; he'd seen it too many times in the heat of battle and had felt God's swift hand. He had to consider that reuniting with September was God at work. Maybe she needed a little help. Maybe he was being given a mission to be that help.

"I always thought it was a great loss that Mom never learned to live or to love again." He kept out his experiences of growing up underneath that dark, hopeless cloud. When his father had died in a logging accident, it was as if he had lost both parents. Understandably, his mother was never the same. But she had never been a mother again. He'd grown up a lonely kid, taking care of his younger sister and finding belonging and acceptance in the neighboring Grangers' house. "I don't think Dad would have wanted her to be alone like she is. He would have wanted her to be happy."

"And you're telling me this because...?"

"We were on the topic. My mom would never have driven me anywhere once, let alone twice, every day of the week." His tone was indifferent, as if his past was something he'd learned to deal with long ago. "Sounds like you have an awfully nice mom."

"We do," Chessie answered, regarding Hawk with a narrow, terse look, which she reserved for possible swindlers and fraudulent door-to-door salesmen. "What I don't get is why you're here. Sure, you were on the search-and-rescue team the base sent out. I get that. But you could have let this go."

"Perhaps I should have." He straightened his shoulders, sitting ramrod in the chair, looking as tough as nails and nobler than any man ever.

"Can't you see this is causing September more pain?" Chessie pushed away from the table and stood, protective older sister and something more. Her distrust was showing. "She shouldn't be reminded of—"

"Stop, Francesca." Her stomach tied up in knots and she took a deep, cleansing breath. "I'm glad Hawk is here. Please don't chase him off."

"I'm going to the grocery store, then." Chessie didn't look happy with her chin set and her mouth clamped into a firm line. "I won't be long. Hawk, I'm guessing you won't be here when I get back. Thank you for finding my sister. And for the pizza."

"Not a problem." He was the kind of man who showed respect, even to a woman being rude to him.

She had to admire him a little more for that. Hawk was a very good man. She simply had to think that and nothing else—the past, Tim or what could have been. She waited until the door had closed behind her sister before she turned back to him. "She's overprotective. I'm sorry."

"She loves her sister. Who can blame her for that?"

At his kindness, the tightness within her chest coiled tighter, cutting off her air. It made no sense why his kindness troubled her more.

"Is it true?" His voice dipped low and comforting. "Is it better for you if I go?"

This was her chance for safety. He was offering her a way out. She could say yes, walk him to the door, thank him for his thoughtfulness and never see him again. The past could remain buried, where it couldn't harm her.

But she had learned to survive. She had become good enough at it to fool everyone else and some days herself. Not today, but some days. Possibly, right now, she could cope instead of simply survive. "No, Hawk. I'm glad you're here. Remember I told you I had wanted to look you up?"

"Sure." He grabbed a napkin from the holder on the table and swiped his mouth and rubbed his hands, looking busy, as if the act was what held his attention, although she could feel his interest, sharp and focused.

"You're here, and this is my chance. I need closure." She thought of the prayers she had given up on and of her need for God's comfort that she had been too lost to feel. Maybe having Hawk here would help as much as anything could. "I'm stronger now than I was after Tim's funeral. Could you tell me what happened to him? Could you tell me how he died? You were there."

"Are you sure you want to hear this?" His hand covered hers, and everything within her stilled.

"Yes." It wasn't the whole truth. She was afraid that it would be better to stay in the dark, to leave the last moments of Tim's life a mystery. She didn't want to hurt again, yet how could she let this chance slip by? Finally she could lay to rest the broken shards of the questions that had troubled her. With the answers, maybe she could have closure.

"I want to know, even if it's difficult." She set her shoulders, braced for the truth. "I know you had been shot, too."

"Caught a ricochet. Nothing serious."

"Can you tell me what he said?"

He didn't answer right away. Moments ticked by and the heater clicked on, breezing warm air across her ankles and teasing the curtains at the window. Hawk sat like a seasoned warrior, his face set, his shadows deepening and his truth unmistakable. He was a man who fought for others and who protected them. He looked every inch of it.

She leaned forward, pulse fluttering, both dreading what he would say and hungering for it.

Chapter Four

❧

"He didn't have a pulse when I got to him." Hawk sounded distant, as if that was the only way he could cope with the memory.

"He was already gone?"

"His brother was closer to him and got there first. He started CPR. The machine guns, the grenades, the shouting, it all faded to silence. Everything went slow motion. I pulled a corpsman over to help because he wasn't coming fast enough."

"You fought for Tim's life." She read the emotion twisting his face and saw what he could not say. This loss had been a turning point in his life, too. "You fought with everything you had."

"We all did." He swallowed hard, the tendons in his neck working with effort. It had to be torture remembering.

She was sorry to put him through that. Maybe she shouldn't have asked. "At least he didn't suffer. That's what I had to know. That he wasn't afraid."

"Tim? Never. We got him back for a minute or so, but the bullet caused too much damage." He reached across the distance separating them, both physical and emotional, to take her hand.

His touch alarmed her. Her spirit flickered and warmed, like dawn's first light. She withdrew her hand, and the brightness dimmed. She sat as if in shadow.

"He gave Pierce a message for his family," he went on as if nothing had happened. "That was all the time he had. He died in his brother's arms and in a circle of friends. The last thoughts he had were of you."

"How do you know?"

"His last breath was your name. Didn't you know?"

She shook her head. She wanted to stay unaffected, to gather the information logically and heal from it. Impossible. Tim's life had ended— all that he would be, all that he would do wiped away. That's what she wanted to change. "If God could give me one wish, I would go back in time and have forced Tim to get out. I would never have let him serve a second hitch in the army. He wouldn't have been sent overseas. He wouldn't have died."

"You don't know that. You can't torture yourself with that guilt."

"How do you know?" She stared at him in amazement, this big, capable man more wise than she had given him credit for.

"I know how you feel," he confessed. "I did everything I could. Everything I knew how. I couldn't save him, either."

Everything within her stilled. Their gazes collided and the force of it left her paralyzed. The honest sincerity of his gaze held a power she had never felt before, one strong enough to chip at the frozen tundra of her shielded heart. "How do you go on?"

"I struggled for a long time." Honesty softened the planes of his rugged face and revealed more of his character. One of strength and deep feeling. "I almost opted out and thought about finding a civilian job."

"You were soul-searching, too."

"Not that I want to admit it to anyone." He squared his shoulders. "I had to question what one life is worth, and what cost? I had a hole in my life as a reminder. I had to figure that Tim would want me to make good choices for me, so I turned down my uncle's offer to find me a job and signed for another two years."

"That was your idea of a good choice? Going back into danger?"

"I want to make a difference."

"There are a lot of ways to do that without risking your life."

"Are you questioning my decision?" Not defensive, but curious. He looked as if he wanted to take hold of her hand again.

She kept them tightly folded together. "I'm just asking, that's all."

"My sister is happily working in San Diego. She doesn't need me. My mom is safe and living her life the way she wants to in Wyoming. They are the only family I have, and neither of them really needs me. I'm not married. I don't have any strong calling to do charity work or anything like that. The military is what I believe in. Being a soldier was the only thing I ever wanted to be."

"Why?" It was Tim's decision she was asking about, not Hawk's. But she had to know why Hawk had chosen to be a Ranger. "Why do you guys feel so committed to the army?"

"Because I fight for what I believe in. I love

this country. I want to do my part." Not defensive, just powerful. Poignant. "Although it comes at a cost. I'm still single."

"Why haven't you gotten married?"

"Why get involved with someone when I knew I had to leave?"

"And yet being alone is the reason you stayed in the army?"

"It's a circular argument. Don't think I don't know that." He shrugged a shoulder, as if dismissing it, but something that looked like sadness clung to his features. "You're alone, too, September. I don't have to ask to know the answer. You aren't dating."

"No. I don't have the heart left to." She couldn't give voice to the loneliness of the last two years and the fears that she had been broken beyond repair. Beyond hope. Beyond God.

"We are two of a kind."

"In some ways," she agreed.

He leaned closer, looking as if he wanted to comfort her and didn't know how.

She was grateful he didn't reach out. It was easier to stay frozen inside than to look toward the light. "Are you going to be here alone for the holidays? Or are you flying home?"

"I haven't decided. I might head down to

Mom's. My sister will be there. It would be good to see them both."

"You haven't said it, but I can hear it. There's something holding you back."

"It's tough going down there. My mom never got over my dad's death. Nearly twenty years later, she lives like a hermit, closed off from what life has to offer." He shifted in his chair. "I love her, and it's hard for me to see. I couldn't save her, either."

"Don't give up on her, Hawk." Sunlight brightened, tumbling through the windows, finding her. The lemony brightness graced her, emphasizing an inner strength, a glimpse into the real September Stevens. "Everyone needs love in their life. Even you."

"Me? When did this conversation become about me?" Sure, he was uncomfortable with the *L* word. He was too tough for love. Too scarred. "I'll go visit my mom for Christmas. Fine. We were talking about you."

"Were we? I don't think it's necessary. I'm fine, too."

"Sure, you look it, bandaged and casted. Don't forget I found you in that hole in the earth. You can't fool me."

"Okay, fine. My arm hurts. My head hurts. I

sat in what felt like a grave and worried about dying."

"I'm glad I found you."

"Me, too."

He would never forget the relief or how it had pounded through him with the force of a riptide, leaving him weak down to the quick. Like now, never had he seen a lovelier sight than her alive. The sunshine clung to her, as if it thought so, too. He was thankful to God for this mercy. "You are going to take care of yourself, right? Need me to get you anything? Do something for you?"

"In case you haven't noticed, I have my sister for that."

"Yeah, well, I was asking as a friend." Okay, so he cared for her. He was man enough to admit it. But it was caring on a nonromantic level. "Don't know about you, but that's something I could use."

"Me, too." She relaxed, as if a wall went down. When she stood, it didn't feel as if she were trying to keep him at a safe distance. "Any man who hauls me out of a mine is a friend for life."

"Glad to hear it." He kept pace with her through the kitchen. Nice and amiable, walking alongside her. "I noticed you have a gutter coming loose from your fascia."

"My what?"

"The board beneath the roofline."

"Oh. No idea. I haven't looked up in a while, but there are a few drips when it rains."

"This is the Pacific Northwest. It tends to rain a lot here. Hello." He was chuckling, knowing full well what she was doing. Downplaying the problem because she knew what was coming next. "There's no avoiding it. We're friends now. You have to accept my help."

"It's a law? Written into the Constitution?"

"I'm sure it is. I'll put it on my to-do list." She wasn't getting rid of him easily. He wasn't a man who walked away from a mission or regrets. He spotted a trio of cardboard boxes next to the big front window. Indentations in the carpet showed that a piece of furniture had been recently moved. "That would make a perfect spot for a Christmas tree."

"Which is why I moved the couch. Don't give me that look. I did it before the accident. Last weekend." She shook her head. "I'm afraid to ask about that expression on your face. You are planning something."

"I'm a planner. It's who I am." He didn't deny

it. Regrets could haunt a man when he was belly down in the sand, taking fire. That meant he couldn't afford to back off now. "Since we're friends and all, I have a few thoughts to help you out while you are down and out."

"In case you haven't noticed, I am getting around just fine. My arm is casted, that's all. The rest of me is good to go."

She tried to hide it, but he wasn't a fool. He knew how loss could strip you of your heart, breaking it off piece by piece until there was no light, no love and no hope left. Sometimes a person needed a hand up, that was all. More than anything he wanted to be that hand for her.

"Getting a tree. Putting up lights. Decorating." He had reached the door and turned, drawing out his time with her. "Seems like doing all that is going to be hard with that cast."

"Then it's a good thing I'm not going to go all-out for Christmas. I'm going to haul out my little plastic tree—"

"Plastic? Sorry. No. I can't allow that."

"The last time I looked, you were not in charge of me." She planted her good arm on her hip. "I'm used to you pushy alpha types. You don't intimidate me, Mark Hawkins."

"I'm not trying to intimidate you." He

grinned, bringing out his dashing twin dimples. He had a smile that could charm glaciers into melting. "I'm helping out a friend. Remember, that's what we are?"

"I owe my life to you. How could I forget?" Yes, he really was far too charming for his good—and hers. "I know what you're up to."

"Just trying to help spread Christmas cheer. Do unto others. Help the less fortunate." He sure *appeared* innocent.

"Sure you are." She could see right through him to the pure kindness beneath. Hard not to appreciate that. "If you really have nothing else to do with your free time."

"I'm on leave. The rest of the year is mine."

He didn't need to say the words, because she understood. He was lonely, too. One of his best friends was gone. She knew just what that was like.

"How about I drop by tomorrow?" He gave the knob a turn. Damp, chilly air puffed into the room. "We'll see if we can do something about your lack of Christmas spirit."

"I may need help." What she needed was a friend. She liked the idea that maybe he needed her.

"Then prepare yourself. I fully intend to put you in a festive mood. Consider it fair warning."

"Yes, Sergeant." She couldn't resist saluting him. He eased onto the front porch, reminding her of the man she'd once lost and the future she was still grappling to find. "You were shot on that mission, but you didn't say where."

"Nothing serious. I healed up okay."

She recognized that hollow sound, for it was the way her voice sounded when the past threatened to overtake her. "What happened? No one has told me."

"First I took a bullet to the shoulder and then shrapnel in my back. A grenade went off nearby and I covered Tim's body with mine to protect him." He waved off the importance, but emotion darkened his eyes. He was not a man to talk of his sacrifices. He had come to the wake, but he'd been more injured than she had realized.

Caring rolled through her, unbidden and impossible to stop.

"I'm glad you recovered, Hawk."

"Until tomorrow." He saluted her in return, pivoted on his heel and marched into the watery sunshine. She thought she caught a hint of hope on his handsome face, but she couldn't be sure.

Good, she thought, because that's how she

felt, too. Hopeful because he was coming back, encouraged at the prospect of seeing him again. Maybe it was because he was familiar, an old acquaintance. She liked the idea of being friends with him. As he strode toward his bike, she remembered the few group outings they had been on together long ago: volleyball at the park, bowling at Tim's favorite rink, a barbecue on base. In all of those memories, Hawk had always been laughing, a dependable guy, a steadfast and loyal friend to the man she'd lost.

She closed the door, and the click echoed in the silent house. She leaned against the door, fighting against falling into the hole of grief she had spent years climbing out of. She could no longer feel God, but she had to believe He was somewhere close. *Lord, I'm trying to move on and let go. I've given my sorrow up to You so many times, too many to count. And yet I'm still holding this burden. It's like being trapped beneath a deep layer of ice. I can't see You to find my way out. A little help, please.*

No answer came, and she didn't expect one. She only hoped her words had a chance of being heard. A motor roared to life outside, muffled by the sturdy walls, and she caught sight of a blur moving beyond the window—Hawk rocketing down the street. She moved to the sill, but he was already gone. Sunshine swept the steady branches of the rhododendrons outside, their green leaves held up toward the sky, as if with faith.

The back door opened and Chessie's shoes clicked on the hardwood. Sacks rustled as they came to rest on the kitchen counter.

"I see he's gone." Her voice echoed in the coved ceiling and bounced off the plain white walls. She clomped into sight. "Tell me why you aren't lying on the couch with your feet up."

"Because I'm bored of lying still. Let me help put away the groceries."

"Not on your life. Get on that couch or do I have to come over there and make you do it?" Chessie might be all bark, but it was concern that softened her dark eyes, worry that furrowed across her brow. "You are my only sister, don't forget. I could have lost you. So, are you going to do what I ask?"

"Yes, big sis." Tired and drained, she re-treated to the couch. It felt good to lie back on the soft cushions and fluffy pillows and grab the remote.

After Chessie was done putting away the gro-ceries, she plopped in the nearby chair. They spent the afternoon watching classic movies and humming along with Fred Astaire. But to her, Hawk wasn't forgotten. He was like those old songs, familiar and dear, the ones she wanted to sing over and over again.

The tree lot on the corner of two main roads sparkled with cheerful Christmas lights rimming their blocked-off portion of the grocery store parking lot. Through the rain speckling the windshield, she spotted an older man and his wife trying to stay dry under a small makeshift awning. It had to be a cold job. She empathized, as she often worked in the cold winter rain, too.

"Looks like we have plenty of choices." Hawk stopped the truck and killed the engine. The hot air from the heater sputtered out, and the windshield immediately began to fog. "We're the only customers here."

"I can't imagine why." She released her seat belt, turning toward him in the seat. Rain pinged on the glass, smearing the outside world like one big Christmas watercolor. "Don't most people shop for trees in the pouring rain?"

"I've been in monsoons that were drier than this," he quipped. "Wait a second. I'll grab an umbrella and come around for you."

"Umbrella? Who do you think I am? I'm a Seattle girl. I'm not afraid of a little rain." She opened her door and hopped down from the truck, lifting her face to the spattering rain.

Footsteps splashed on the wet blacktop, pounding in her direction. Hawk, glowering at her, as he rounded the front corner of the truck.

"You could have waited for me to help you down." He stared at the umbrella, folded and tied neatly in hand. "It's too late for this now. You're already dripping wet and loving it."

"After being cooped up indoors for so many days, I do love it." She swiped at the raindrops collecting on her lashes and breathed in the fresh-cut tree scent. "I'm feeling better already."

"You look better. There's color in your cheeks."

"See? I don't need to be pampered. Too bad my sister isn't here to see. I'm going stir-crazy." She waved to the couple huddled under their awning. "Good morning."

"Hello there," the husband greeted. "Are you two wanting anything in particular?"

"We'll browse around and let you know." Hawk stepped in, locking his arm through her good one. They must look like a couple out to buy their tree. "Where do you want to start?

There's some good-looking spruce right here. Well shaped and full. That would look mighty pretty in your front window."

"I would rather shop around first. See what my options are."

"That's where we are different. I know what I want and when I see it, I grab it and go. Quick in and quick out."

"The Ranger way?" She shook her head, enjoying the pleasant squish of puddled water beneath her boots and the symphony of rainfall pattering around them. Holiday lights flashed cheerfully as she followed an aisle past the perfect trees. "I like to take a careful look. Sometimes you find a hidden treasure."

"I see what you mean." His tone was thoughtful, drawing her attention. Suddenly she didn't feel as if he was talking about the trees surrounding them.

Heat stained her face, and she looked away. With every step she took, she was deeply aware of him at her side. The force of his noble presence was as tangible as the ground beneath her feet.

"How about this one?" He paused to admire a noble fir, tall and proud and perfect.

"It is lovely." She bit her bottom lip, a habit

when she was thinking. "I can't help but think this tree is gorgeous. Any number of people will want it. It will sell in a snap."

"Well, I don't know. It's still here, isn't it?"

"It's two weeks before Christmas. A lot of people haven't come by yet. I'm positive this tree will find a home."

"So that means we get it?" He wasn't exactly paying attention to her every word. He couldn't. She captivated him, looking like Christmas come early with her spun-sugar pink hat, scarf and mittens and matching coat.

"It means I feel confident leaving the tree right here."

"Right. Because we have to worry about the trees who won't find a home?" A total guess on his part, but he knew he was right when he was rewarded by her smile.

"Now you're getting it, Hawkins." She took the lead. "I'll take point. Follow me."

"You've picked up a few military terms." He jammed his fists into his coat pockets and trailed after her.

"Hard not to. C'mon, soldier. I see exactly what I'm looking for." She forged ahead, undaunted by the virtual forest surrounding them, sure of her mission.

"I know what you are up to." He hiked to keep up with her. "You are going for the pity tree."

"Pity tree? I don't think that's a very nice thing to say. Trees are God's creations and every one of them is beautiful." She tossed a grin over her shoulder, as if daring him to argue.

As if he could argue with the likes of her. Too pretty and smart for a guy like him—besides, she made any arguments vanish. How could any guy argue with her? When she smiled, she made his heart skip three beats, but he didn't break stride as he caught up to her. He shook his head. "I should have known."

"This one is perfect." She touched a scrawny branch of the slightly lopsided Douglas fir. He'd never seen a sorrier tree—or at least not one that was still green.

"I'm not even going to try to talk you out of it." He might not be the smartest tool in the shed, but he knew happiness when he saw it. He wouldn't take that from her for the world. "You're sure this is the one you want? There might be a more sickly looking one on the other side of the lot."

"I've bonded with this one. Plus, it's a live tree." She pointed to the big brown planter, presumably of all natural material.

"Perfect."

"I'm glad you think so. You're more of a kindred spirit than I first thought." She beamed up at him, a moment of joy on a rainy gray day, and his heart did more than skip a few beats. Everything within him stilled, as if he would never be the same.

"Can I help you with that?" The owner appeared with a handcart.

Hawk hardly heard him. In the whimsical flash of the multicolored twinkle lights, September's gaze locked on his with appreciation, and guilt hit him like a cluster bomb.

Chapter Five

The cotton candy clouds slowly ripped apart, and the rain turned to a lazy drizzle as she let Hawk help her into the truck. His hand at her elbow was a comfort. She felt better today than she had in a long time. Maybe it had to do with getting out of the house and feeling the wonder of the outdoors, the rugged, snowcapped mountains rimming the horizon. Maybe—just maybe—it had to do with the man who pulled her seat belt for her and buckled her in snuggly.

"Tell me why you aren't married again?" He was a gentleman and a caretaker. She had a soft spot for the protective, caring type.

"No woman will have me." He grinned, flashing those gorgeous dimples of his as if he knew full well the effect they had on a girl. "Probably because I'm deployed all the time. Hard to know a girl long enough that she could see past my faults."

"Your *numerous* faults," she couldn't resist correcting.

"Hey! I'm not that bad. At least, I hope not." He winked, confident as always, and closed the door. Even through the blur of the wet windshield, he radiated integrity and good humor. Definitely hard not to like the guy.

The door wrenched open and he hopped behind the wheel. "I hope you're not keeping count of my faults."

"I've decided to make a list."

"That's bound to be one mighty long list." He laughed at that and started the truck.

A list. That might do it. She would need some way to keep from liking him too much. Hard to say why, but she felt more herself today. She could almost see the girl she used to be in the reflection of the shadowy windshield.

"Anything you need to get? Any place you need to go?" He put the truck in Reverse and laid his arm over the back of the bench seat dangerously close to her. "Maybe new decorations for your new tree?"

Sitting there, with the defroster blowing through his short, dark hair and happiness softening the striking planes of his masculine face, he represented everything noble and righteous in the world. His honor shone through, unmistakable. She saw friendship and kindness and a soldier's loyalty. She had the feeling that if she asked him, he would move the mountains stone by stone.

"There is somewhere I'm dying to go." She pointed to the right—away from the way home—after he turned the truck around. "I need to see my horse."

"I thought doctor's orders were to take it easy. You might not have been hurt the way Crystal was, but you're bruised up pretty good. I know. Back at the hospital, I sweet-talked the nurses into telling me the truth." Serious concern layered the deep notes of his voice and warmed the air between them. Not accusing, when he could be, and not controlling when he could simply drive her home. He probably had no idea how attractive that made him. His gaze fastened on hers, as if he were expecting nothing short of the whole truth. "Do you feel up to it?"

"Not exactly. I'm still fairly weak." His gaze intensified, or maybe it was her perception. She resisted the urge to tear away and break the intimacy. "I've heard the reports, I've spoken to my boss and the vet, but I have to see with my own eyes that Comanche is okay. He's been my best friend for the last ten years."

"Friendship means a lot to you."

"It's everything." Friendship was the kind of love she could depend on. She fingered her cast, fighting frustration. "I miss him. Whatever has gone wrong in my life, Comanche has always been there to make it easier. And now I can't drive because of the medication I'm on, so I can't see him."

"What about your sister? Won't she drive you?"

"Chessie tends to be a little overprotective."

"A big sister's prerogative." He hit the turn signal—right, not left toward home. "Here's the deal—no riding, no stress and strain, no exertion of any kind."

"*Thank* you, Hawk." Hard not to like him more than she already did. Joy sparkled through her, and it was because of him. "You never answered my question."

"Neatly evaded it, did I? Learned how to walk softly in Ranger School. It's saved me more than once."

"You can't tiptoe around this ambush. I have skills of my own. Being a riding instructor teaches you a lot of things. Perseverance. Focus. How to stick with a problem until you work out a solution." She liked how tiny lines crinkled at the corners of his eyes when he grinned.

"So you're saying I have met my match?"

"You have. No more glib phrases so you don't have to face the real issue."

"I'm in big trouble." He slowed to a stop at the intersection and let his eyes meet hers. "Okay, here's the scoop. I'm not looking for marriage right now for the same reason you haven't started dating again."

"Oh." She didn't want to look at the places iced over and wintry within her, but she understood. He didn't need to say more. "Tim."

"I don't want to leave someone behind to grieve me." He checked for traffic and concentrated overly hard on his driving, as if the simple task of making a right-hand turn took all of his mental capabilities.

Caring. That was the danger. She understood what he could not say. That when you took the initial small step in a relationship, you let that person through your first layer of defenses. When you cared, you opened your heart, leaving you vulnerable to the world, to life and to loss. Sometimes that was too much of a risk to take.

The swipe of the wiper against the windshield helped to fill the silence between them. Miles rolled by in many shades of green—the faded tones of the grass, the deeper hues of the evergreens, the sedate greens of bushes and shrubbery. Houses on acreage whisked by and within minutes she was pointing at the turnoff to the riding stables.

"Is this the same place where you learned to ride as a kid?" he asked as he parked in the gravel lot.

"Yes. When I was ten, I used to makes wishes on the first star of the night that I would grow up to be just like Colleen. She owns the stables. I couldn't imagine spending my life working with horses and riding all day." She reached to release her seat belt, but he beat her to it.

"Just proves some dreams are meant to come true." He released the buckle, his hand catching hers. The calm of the contact shook her. It lasted only for a moment before he turned away. "This time you wait for me to come help you down. I know I don't look like it, but I can be a gentleman."

"I never doubted it." The door shut, leaving

her alone in the compartment. He dominated her thoughts. He was all she could see as he circled around and opened her door. His hand took hers again, and she leaned into his touch, wanting more of the unyielding peace he brought to her. She wasn't sure the exact moment her feet touched the ground.

"Tell me what you do here besides private lessons." He beeped his truck locked and followed her across the gravel toward the main barn. "Did you used to show?"

"Now I train others who show. But don't get me wrong. I spend a lot of hours mucking stalls and hauling hay. Barn work is a part of owning a horse." She strode through the main doors, open to the blustery winds, and hiked down the aisle. Gladness radiated from her, and she raised her good hand to someone out of his sight and kept going. "I practically live here. I'm never home."

"I know what that's like." He loved his job, too, the challenge and the duty. This was a different world, one that smelled like fresh alfalfa and horse. A pleasant combination, one that drew up memories of his boyhood in Wyoming, racing through the fields of wild grasses, while across the way farmers cut their fields, the scent carrying on the summer breeze. On either side of him, horses poked their heads over their gates, full of curiosity. Everything was clean and shining, from the polished wood to the animals themselves.

"There's my boy." A horse whinnied, more anxious than the others at the sight of the woman in the aisle, and she went to him. Her good hand curled around his fancy purple halter. "Hey, Comanche. I've been missing you, big fella."

Hawk froze in the aisle, caught by the sight of the petite woman, diminutive compared to the giant gold horse. The animal strained against the gate, making it groan as he pressed his face into her hand. He nibbled the edge of her cast as if with great concern.

"It's all right. I can still ride." Her assurance was met with a doubting nicker.

He could watch the woman all day long. She was different with her horse, softer, more alive and less shadowed. Her hair hung in a straight curtain, framing her sweetheart's face, and she moved like a Christmas carol—with grace and spirit. She leaned her forehead against the horse's cheek, a moment of pure tenderness between two friends.

That was what it would be like to be close to her, he realized. Sugarcoated moments and quiet closeness. His heart warmed as feelings came to life, new and powerful and unlike anything he'd known before. Soft and tender emotions, ones he had no right to. He more than cared about her. He liked her. A lot. Guilt returned to pierce him like a blade.

"He's a good-looking horse." What he knew about the creatures could fit into a boot, but it didn't take a horseman to see the quality of the animal. His face was finely shaped, his forehead high and intelligent, his eyes wise and kind. His coat gleamed like honey in sunshine, and his mane shimmered like white silk. Beneath the purple blanketlike garment he wore, the horse looked pleasingly built.

"Comanche has an impressive pedigree. A quality quarter horse isn't cheap. I think my parents took out a second mortgage on their house for him and the mare they bought my sister when we were in junior high."

"Good parents."

"The best." She readily agreed, and she had never looked lovelier or more wholesome, the kind of woman a man wanted to come home to. She could make a soldier like him wish for things that were out of his reach.

He winced, wanting to retreat. He had no right feeling this way. He was wrong to look at September and wish.

"My sister mostly grew out of her horse phase, but I never will." Her laughter rippled, the sound of gentle chiming joy, as the horse lapped at her coat pocket, trying to work it open. Gently, she focused her attention on Comanche. "Let me see what I have in here. I might be out of peppermint."

They were a pair, Hawk decided as he watched woman and horse. September bent to her task, her hair hiding her face as she searched in her pocket and came up with a single wrapped piece of candy. Best friends, she had said. He didn't doubt that the horse adored her. Being close to her had to be as sweet as walking in heaven.

"This is the only one, sorry, buddy." She unwrapped the candy, while the horse tried to grab it with his whiskery lips. When he succeeded, she laughed again, a sound that wrapped around Hawk's heart, a memory he would never let go of.

His quiet, unspoken wish remained, right and wrong all at once. Torture. He cleared his throat, struggling to hide it. "I bet there isn't anything Comanche doesn't know about you."

"True. He is my closest confidant."

"So, if I want to learn your secrets, I would have to go to him. Get him to talk." He ambled closer and rubbed the gelding's nose. Comanche crunched happily on his candy.

"Why? Is there something you want to know about me?" She cast him a sideways glance, curiosity alight on her delicate features.

"Don't worry. Your secrets are safe. I don't speak horse."

"Lucky for me." She dipped her head, as if suddenly shy.

Maybe because he was studying her too boldly. He didn't mean to. She had hints of little dimples, and he missed seeing her real smile, the full-fledged, all-out one he remembered back when she had been dating Tim. What would it take to see that full-out grin again? Everything within him longed for the sight.

Guilt wedged again into his soul. What would Tim think? Was his buddy looking down from heaven right now with anger? Or would he understand? Hawk shifted his weight, stepping away, and the horse nickered in protest. Apparently Comanche was used to a lot of adoration.

September had turned to him, about to speak, when someone called her name. She whipped around, her hair flying, calling out a howdy to the woman bouncing down the aisle.

"I knew you couldn't stay away!" A redhead wrapped September in a careful hug. "Everyone has been asking about you and wanting to know when you're coming back."

"As soon as the doctor says I can."

The two women fell into a lively conversation about people and horses. Hawk leaned against Comanche's stall and folded his arms. September was all he could see—the graceful, tall way she stood like a ballet dancer. Her warm manner, her concern for the other people she discussed with the redhead, her gentle voice that had the nearby horses turning their heads to listen to her. Could he blame them? Not one bit.

Face it, you like her, man. And not just a little, either. If only he knew how to bury his affection for her or to somehow erase his feelings. He had no right to them. None at all.

Peace. It seeped into her in an innocent warm rush that went straight to her heart. September took one last look at the stables—a comforting place where she truly belonged—before Hawk turned the truck around and headed down the drive. "At least the rain has stopped."

"I hadn't noticed."

"I was afraid of that." She rolled her eyes at the amusement in his voice. Of course she hadn't meant to stay so long. "You have gone numb with boredom, haven't you? Chessie is always quick to tell me how monotonous it is to wait when I'm in my horse zone."

"Trust me, I wasn't bored." A sheepish curve of his mouth did intriguing things to his dimples.

Not that she was noticing. "How could you not be? I shouldn't have yakked on like that. Once I get going, I can't seem to stop. It's like time isn't passing. I'm sorry. How can I make it up to you?"

"I'll think of something. After all, I *did* suffer."

"So now you change your story? When there's something to be gained?"

"Call it curiosity." He hit the turn signal and checked for traffic. "You can't fault me for being inquisitive."

"How does a homemade dinner sound?"

"I wouldn't turn that down. I'm not the typical bachelor. I can cook for myself. The trouble is that I don't like to cook for one. Something tells me you are a good cook."

"I'm fair to middling." She leaned back against the seat, already looking forward to it. "I should be up to it tomorrow. I suppose a handsome bachelor like you has plans for a Saturday night."

"Are you kidding? I'm as free as a bird."

"You say that with a grin. You don't have any solid plans at all?"

"I'm usually pretty scheduled. Since I'm on leave, I want to hang loose. Take it as it comes. See where the road takes me." He accelerated across the lanes of traffic and merged into the flow of the other cars. "I'm a free spirit."

"I've noticed." She tried to recall what she knew about Hawk. Somewhere in the recesses of her mind, she remembered Tim saying he always went for action sports. "You like skiing, right? Plan on doing any while you're a free spirit?"

"I've got a few trips planned. A buddy of mine and I are heading to Canada to do a climb."

"You mean as in scaling a mountain?"

"No, the glacier. Ice climbing."

"If I were you, I would head south. Find sunshine and a warm beach."

"Tempting, but I've decided to stick around here. Who says life isn't adventurous around you? I'm curious to see what happens next."

"Me, too." She laughed, deep and true, and it felt good. "I'm not sure I can compete with extreme skiing or inching up a glacier with an ice pick, but I make a great pot of spaghetti and meatballs."

"Are you kidding? I got a good view of you back at the stables."

"A good view of me?" She hardly noticed the yards and trees flashing by, or the fact that she was almost home. He intrigued her. His presence filled the truck's cab, overwhelming her. A smart girl would keep him at a distance.

"It's who you are, with your horse and your friends. It's a dream you had as a little girl, spending your time with your horse, learning all you could about riding. Your friends are there. Your life is there. You want your future there, exactly the same way it's been. You fit at that stable. You can be the woman you were meant to be."

"Yes. How did you know?" She felt her jaw drop. She stared at him, astonished.

"It fits with your beliefs. You wear your causes on your T-shirts."

"I am a fan of the ride and walkathons." She looked down at her blue shirt; the white lettering read Race for Childhood Diabetes. "Comanche and I like to do our part. Next week there's a ride for the local food bank. It's not ice climbing, but it might be fun."

"I'll do it, but I don't have a horse."

"No worries. I can find you a mount."

"I *knew* you were going to say that. I guess there's no way out now." He didn't look too broken up by it.

His gentle friendliness was hard to resist. Through the permanent layers of ice she had been buried in, he reached her. She was helpless to stop his gentle breach of her defenses. His grin, his dimples, his friendliness, his understanding, his willingness to ride along touched her deeply. A true caring took root within her, and she could not stop it.

"Count me in." He pulled into her driveway. The sun broke, piercing ragged gray clouds as if in victory. He cut the engine.

Like the sun, her feelings were too intense. She blinked against the brightness and unlatched her seat belt before he could do it. Overwhelmed, she struggled to keep him at a distance, but her emotions weren't cooperating.

She had to stop the caring from taking firmer root in her heart.

"There you are." Her sister stormed down the walkway, mouth pursed, and anger flashing. "I've been worried about you. No note. Nothing. Your car in the garage. What was I supposed to think?"

"I didn't know you were coming over." She hopped down from the seat and spotted Chessie's sedan in the nearby guest parking spot. "I didn't mean to worry you."

"Too late." Chessie sent an accusing glance Hawk's way. "You. I should have known you had something to do with this. I suppose you let her talk you into going to the stables?"

"Guilty. She's hard to say no to." Hawk did look guilty as he unlatched the tailgate. "I didn't keep her out long."

"She has a concussion. She's had surgery. She can't be out running around with the likes of you." Chessie stopped herself, just in time. "I'm sorry. I'm grateful to you for finding her. I always will be. But she's fine now. She doesn't need another soldier messing up her life."

"Francesca." September's face burned. She took a step toward her sister, then realized how alone Hawk looked as he hauled the tree out of the truck bed. How miserable as he wrapped his arms around the planter and lifted. Tendons strained in his neck—it had to be heavy. "Hawk, let me get the door for you."

"You might want to find something to put under this. You don't want this on your pretty wood floor." He sounded strained, and the branches hid him effectively. It was hard to read the emotion on his face.

She didn't need to see him to know he'd been hurt. "Chessie, will you find something?"

Her sister gave her a long look, as if she were about to refuse, but decided better of it. She meant well, September thought as she followed her sister onto the porch, but Chessie's strong opinions had a way of always hurting someone. She was too much like their dad—a good soul, but so sure her way was the only one.

"You've done me a world of good today." September held the door for him and her perfectly imperfect Christmas tree. "Don't forget that. I'm grateful, Hawk."

"You did me a world of good, too." He ambled in on a ray of sunshine. He didn't meet her gaze. Something had changed. Maybe it was what Chessie said, or maybe he felt this, too—the growing closeness between them.

Perhaps he wasn't comfortable with that, either. She searched for something to say in the beats of silence between them. Chessie saved her, marching into the room like a field general with an extralarge serving platter she'd found in the kitchen.

"Right here?" Hawk asked, his voice hooking her attention.

"Yes. Perfect." She hardly noticed where her sister placed the platter and Hawk settled the tree. Sunshine tumbled through the window, growing brighter, and gracing the man who turned the planter to show off the fir.

Hawk was a thoughtful man. He had become a loner, too, just as she had. Somehow Chessie had left the room, she hadn't noticed that, either, leaving them alone. The pleasant afternoon, their conversation and closeness remained between them.

"If you've changed your mind about supper tomorrow, I would understand." He jammed his fists into his coat pockets, attempting to seem casual.

She wasn't fooled. It had to be an effort for him, as it was for her. Their wounded pasts stood between them, something that could not be erased or forgotten.

"No way, soldier. You are coming tomorrow. End of story." She owed him that much. She couldn't risk caring about him, but she wasn't about to toss him out in the cold, either. Hadn't he admitted today had helped him, too? Maybe there was a higher purpose at work—and that thought surprised her. She hadn't looked to her faith in a long time. She followed him to the door. "I'm going to need help with the tree. I can't decorate by myself."

His grin said he saw straight through her. He glanced toward the kitchen—must be where Chessie had retreated to—but he didn't point out the obvious, that she was hardly alone. Instead, he hesitated on the porch and peered up at the gutters. "I'll bring my toolbox and see if I can't get that patched for you."

"That would be nice of you, Hawk."

"Not nice, trust me." He looked like a man struggling as he lifted a hand. "See you tomorrow."

"Come anytime," she called after him. She wasn't sure if she caught a grim downturn to his mouth, or if it were simply a trick of the light. He bounded away, a powerful, substantial man.

What a relief. She eased into the house and closed the door. Through the window, she could see his truck door close and pale exhaust puff into the damp, cold air. Since he was leaving, she could return to her peaceful numbness, to let her feelings settle into nothingness. She could go back to the way she'd been.

"I don't like how he looks at you." Chessie returned with two steaming cups, tea bag tags dangling.

"What are you talking about? Hawk looks at me with respect."

"Exactly. You aren't going to get involved with him, are you?"

"How could you think such a thing?" As if. She wasn't that girl, not anymore. "Nothing happened. Nothing's changed."

"Are you sure about that?"

Staying silent, September turned to the window in time to catch sight of Hawk's truck ambling down the road, and her spirit brightened. She was wrong—everything had changed. She had changed. Hawk had stirred her emotions to life and there was no going back.

Chapter Six

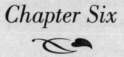

Why couldn't he get her out of his mind? He'd been home for hours, but the five-mile jog and the hour's worth of chores had not pushed her from his thoughts. She remained front and center and nothing he did could dislodge the sweet memories of how she had looked in that stable, her uninjured arm around her horse. Her girl-next-door beauty and gentle nature had caught him like a fish on a hook.

He dropped the laundry basket in front of the dryer and opened the door. No way could he deny how he felt about her. He knelt, reaching in for his fresh, warm laundry. As towels tumbled into the basket, he battled something that went beyond guilt. If Tim knew, what would he think? Should he walk away?

"What are you doing here, Hawk?" Reno,

a fellow Ranger, plodded into the basement laundry room with a full basket in his arms. "I thought you were on leave?"

"Still have to do laundry regardless." He knew that wasn't what his buddy meant. He closed the dryer door, caught the basket with the side of his boot and scooted it over to the next dryer. "Haven't gotten around to heading out of town."

"What is it this time? Extreme skiing? Base jumping?" Reno set his burden on top of a washer. Typically, he was wearing an army T-shirt and battered jeans, just like Hawk. "I heard you and Granger were up to something."

"We've got a date with a mountain up north, and a backcountry trip in Wyoming." He tugged open the dryer. "That ought to keep me out of trouble."

"Or in it." Reno smirked and upended his basket into a washer. "Only two scheduled activities? I don't get Granger. Once you tie yourself up with a woman, your fun gets curtailed. That's why I'm a free man."

"That's not why you don't have a gorgeous fiancée." Hawk couldn't resist. Joking with one's buddies was the Ranger way. "It's your personality, man. No woman would have you."

"Hey, I could get a fiancée if I wanted one. Girls would line up to marry me."

"Right. I'll try not to trip over the long line on my way out." His basket full, he headed for the exit. "Dude, there's only one reason you and I are doing laundry on a Friday night."

"I've got a ten-mile run first thing in the morning." Reno boasted. "Got to keep in killer shape. The ladies can't resist that."

"You're a sad man, Reno." He shook his head with mock pity. "Destined to be a lonely bachelor."

"Hey, you're doing laundry, too." Reno's laughter filled the stairwell. "I'm not alone in the sad department."

No denying that. With a grin, Hawk took the staircase, rounded the landing and kept climbing. His footsteps made a lonely sound. His buddy's good-natured banter stuck with him. They were two confirmed bachelors—at least in this stage of life—and since he wasn't one to hang out in bars or play dating games, he was doing chores on a Friday night. He used to hang out with Pierce, but Pierce was in Wyoming with his fiancée, the lucky dog.

That was one reason he had considered getting out. He didn't have the kind of faith in love that Pierce did. No way could he leave a woman behind over and over again, knowing what distance and constant separation could do to a relationship. He didn't want to take that chance. No, it was better to wait, at least that's what he told himself as he unlocked his door and dropped the laundry on his couch. He didn't want to admit his heart had ideas of its own.

September. The light floral scent of her shampoo and lotion had somehow gotten on his shirt, and he couldn't forget her. The image of her, tall and slim and graceful, trailed after him as he ambled into the kitchen. The music of her laughter, the warmth of her joy, the way she picked out Christmas trees and tried to save the world riding and walking for one cause after another. Emotions swelled within him, pure and honest tenderness.

He was in trouble. He opened the mayonnaise jar, knifed some on the bread lying on a plate and finished making his sandwich. A smart man would end it right here. He would never turn around and look back, but keep going forward without another thought of the woman.

You know that's the right thing, he told himself. He slapped slice after slice of roast beef on the bread, then went for the cheese. The

Lord knew he had enough to keep him busy. He didn't want any emotional entanglements, so he should stop these feelings. Do what it took to break the connection he felt with her.

He layered lettuce and tomato on his sandwich and reached for the mustard jar. That settled it. Tomorrow, he would help with September's decorations and do a few minor repairs around the house, but he would keep a tight rein on his feelings. Sure, it would be tough, but he was a Ranger. He was tougher.

Satisfied, he moved his sandwich to a plate, grabbed a bag of chips and headed to the couch.

September heard the knock over the sizzling meatballs. She turned down the heat, checked on the bubbling tomato sauce and grabbed a towel to wipe her fingers. She hurried to the door, feeling both anticipation and dread. The tree looked lonely without decorations as she passed by, but that would be soon remedied. She found him on her doorstep, looking dapper in a black leather jacket, matching T-shirt and jeans.

"I brought dessert." He held a baker's box in both hands, and on top lay a bouquet of baby pink roses. "Decided I ought to show up with something besides my tool chest."

"And the flowers?"

"Those are to make you smile."

"Is it working?"

"Prettiest smile I've ever seen. So, yes." He handed her the bouquet, carefully wrapped in florist's paper.

Why this man? Why did her heart flutter when their fingers brushed? "Come in. I've got to get back to the stove."

"Fine. I'll make myself useful out here for a bit."

"Let me know if you need anything. I've got tea water simmering."

"I'll keep that in mind." He set the box on the entry table, a man on a mission. His red toolbox waited for him, and he seemed eager to get to it.

Since the meatballs needed a turn and the sauce a stir, she admired the flowers on her return route to the kitchen. The little pink rosebuds were perfect, not romantic, not casual, just right. She spotted a florist's card tucked into the paper and tugged it loose.

Ecclesiastes 11:7.

She couldn't place it. Since the meat was sizzling, she laid the flowers and card on the counter and grabbed a pair of tongs. Just in time—the meatballs were perfectly browned, and she turned them. Over the drone of the stove exhaust and the popping and crackling oil, she heard the rhythmic beat of a hammer.

Hawk. What was she going to do about him? Before he'd walked back into her life, she had been buried in the past, she believed she might never find her way out. But she had been wrong. He had shown her that.

After giving the sauce a stir, she went in search of her Bible, tucked in with her books on the table. She flipped through the thin, dog-eared pages until she found Ecclesiastes. The hammering stopped as she began to read. *Truly the light is sweet, and a pleasant thing it is for the eyes to behold the sun.*

The door squeaked open, and she didn't need to hear the pad of his boots on the hardwood to know he was coming. She felt his closeness like a touch to her soul. By the time he rounded the corner, she'd put her Bible away and was reaching with her good arm for the teakettle.

"Smells good in here." He took the kettle from her. "Are you sure you should be doing all this? I'm just about ready to take over and order you to the couch."

"Just try taking over my kitchen, soldier." She felt featherlight as she held up two tea boxes for him to choose. He pointed at the mint blend. "I don't relinquish my command easily."

"You could delegate." He filled the two waiting cups on the counter, not bothering to wait for the tea bags. "I've got a few domestic skills."

"We'll see about that." She plopped the bags in the steaming water, pretending to size him up. "I have an order for you. Are you ready?"

"Lay it on me. Whatever it is I can take it." He drew his shoulders back, military posture.

Show-off, September thought, and in the best possible way. He was exemplary and growing in her estimation with every passing moment. Not that she was letting it affect her, because that would be foolish. This was totally casual. She tried not to see anything but a friend standing in her kitchen. A friend. Tim's friend. Reminding herself of Tim ought to make the tension within her ease.

It didn't.

"The pot needs water, if you please. I can't lift it." She found a vase in a bottom cabinet.

"As you wish, pretty lady." He grabbed the pot off the counter next to the sink and hit the tap. Over the rush of water, he kept talking. "Have I told you how impressed I am? It takes a strong woman to rebuild her life."

"If that's how it looks, then I'm glad. It's what I've been trying to do. Go through the motions every day, put one foot in front of the other. Eventually life would get better. If I lived as if it were normal, then maybe one day it might be." She turned off the water for him. "You didn't come here to hear about this."

"Sure I did. We're friends, September. I care." His words grew tender, personal, everything she was afraid of. Her pulse lurched, but before she could move away, he was the one who broke the distance. He carried the pot to the stove and twisted on the burner. "You have a nice home, a job you love, friends who treasure you. I saw all those flowers at the hospital. When you were missing, a lot of people were really scared for you."

"I've done the best I could without my heart." Her throat closed, making it impossible to speak. *Until you,* she wanted to say, *I think you are bringing me back.*

How could she say something like that? It would sound romantic, as if she had a crush on him. She searched, but could not find the words to tell him the difference his friendship had already made for her.

"Your heart is still here." Hawk came to her

and cupped her face in his calloused hands. Absolute certainty blazed in his intense gaze.

Feelings, powerful and overwhelming, winked to life. Her throat clogged tighter, making it impossible to breathe. She felt as if she were falling, but she stood on solid ground. The sauce still bubbled, the oven beeped that it had finished preheating, and the roses on the counter added a delicate fragrance to the air—those things remained the same.

Inside she felt as if the frost within her cracked apart one painful break at a time. The defenses had kept her safe after she lost Tim, and without them she felt as if she might crack apart with them. Except for Hawk's presence. His hands cradled her face with caring reverence, a link that held her together. Thank the Lord for the blessing of friendship.

"How did you do it?" Her voice sounded thin and raw. "You've lost close friends. You've seen suffering and war and terrible things. Yet you are centered and vital. Alive. It's as if none of that has touched you."

"Of course it has. I am a different man because of it." His thumbs stroked her jawline in small comforting circles. "I don't take the good moments for granted. I treasure friendships, respect the hardships other people go through and I'm grateful for every moment. I try to live my life in honor of the friends I have lost."

"How do you deal with the hurt?"

"The way anyone does. I face it and go on."

"With honor." She smiled a little, as if she didn't need to be told that was the Ranger way. "That's what I'm trying to do, but I feel as if I'm groping in the dark."

"That's the sure sign you're doing it right. The right path is never the easiest." He did his best to keep a barrier around his feelings. He was here to help her, nothing more, because it was the right thing. "No gain without pain. It's always darkest before the dawn."

"You're a fount of wisdom."

"Just repeating what I've heard. You're painting me to be someone I'm not. Someone better." He was like anyone else, with more hang-ups than he wanted, just trying to make good decisions and live right. "That doesn't mean I haven't questioned everything from God's motives to my role in the military."

"You mentioned leaving the military."

"I lost a lifelong friend. He died right in front of me. It was a loss that hit hard." He stopped to shore up his defenses and keep his emotions rock steady. "It took me a lot of soul-searching to figure out that I can't be less than who God meant me to be. Holding myself back because of grief, or choosing a path that might not be right for me because I don't want to hurt like that again, is not doing justice to the life God gave me."

"That's what troubles me most." She looked even prettier in her sincerity. She was vulnerable and exposed, and it was easy to see the real September Stevens. He winced. She tugged at every emotion in him, but he had to stand firm.

"I have been doing my best, but I've only been existing. Surviving." Her throat worked, as if she were struggling with emotions, too. "Until you."

"I've done nothing, September. Unless you count the gutter work."

"Go ahead and deny it, but what you have done for me is no joke." She resonated with gratitude and caring.

Easy to read the shine of emotion, for she was an open book to him. With her cinnamon-brown locks curling from the warm kitchen, and her cheeks pink from heightened emotion, it took all his reserve to release her and step away. Letting go of her was the last thing he wanted, but he did it. Instead of drawing her into his arms and holding her close, instead of lifting her chin and capturing her mouth with his, he backed away.

"The water is boiling, and my toolbox is waiting. I've got a few more things to fix. Are you okay?" He fisted his hands to keep from reaching for her.

"Better." She squared her slim shoulders, looking stronger than he had ever seen her.

It wasn't right, it wasn't what he wanted, but he couldn't stop from caring. From truly caring. Right now he would stop the earth from spinning if it would guarantee her happiness.

"I'll be back to dump that pot for you." He turned on his heel, retreating. A smart soldier knew when to head for high ground. "You had better give me a shout when the noodles are done."

"Yes, sir." She saluted him, a twinkle glimmering in her eyes. The hint of her dimples had the force of a grenade attack.

A bigger chunk of guilt dug like shrapnel in his chest, and he headed for safety. There was a lightbulb out in the entryway. He would concentrate on getting that problem solved and repair the damage to his defenses. The evening wasn't over yet.

* * *

Good thing Hawk kept the conversation light throughout the meal. Their honest encounter left her raw and vulnerable, as if a rift had been made in her defenses. She needed to regroup and get used to the change in her. He regaled her with funny stories of him and his buddies, from tent life to travel near disasters and tales of his friendship with other Rangers. He probably thought he was entertaining her—no doubt about it, he was hilarious.

But she got a thorough view of the real Mark Hawkins—loyal, devoted, ever resourceful. A man who never let his friends down. She felt honored to be one of his friends.

He insisted they put on a Christmas CD and sang in harmony while they did the dishes. Bing Crosby serenaded them as they took the bakery box of brownies into the living room and started stringing the tree lights. She told him of her students and a typical day at the stables. He asked about the trail rides she took her students on and the upcoming benefit ride-a-thon. She asked about his sister, who sold real estate, and he asked her about her sister, who was unmarried also.

By the time the multicolor lights were strung

around the tree, she felt on stable ground again. Maybe this was the way things between them should stay—on the surface, casual, nothing too personal. Safer, she opened one of the storage boxes to find a beautiful wreath on top—she and Chessie had made it at a day workshop at a local crafts store.

"Let me guess, you made that." Hawk grabbed another brownie from the box—his third—and took a bite. "You are one of those talented people, aren't you? You probably had never made a wreath before."

"Not a wreath, no." She held it up, deciding it did have a certain festive flare. "This was my only decoration last year. I figured, why bother? My sister and I flew down to Mom's for the whole week."

"Is that what you're doing this year?" Hawk took a second bite of the brownie—gone—and took the wreath.

"This year Mom's husband is taking her for a Mediterranean cruise. She's always wanted to go."

"What about you?"

"Dad and his wife live in Seattle, so we will celebrate up there with them." She removed a box of ornaments from the storage bin. Gold and silver winked in the light. "Work is light around Christmastime. Most people are busy with family and getting ready for the holidays."

"So you will have some time off?" He grabbed his hammer and a nail from his box. "Something tells me you will be at the stables anyway. I saw you yesterday. It's tough on you to stay away."

"My best friend lives there, remember?" She took out an ornament and approached the tree, studying it speculatively. She gave it some thought, as she apparently did everything, before hanging it. "When do you leave for your ice climbing trip?"

"Tomorrow." He didn't like to think about it. Usually he would be gung ho, itching to go and ready to roll. But heading up north meant he wouldn't be with September. Nope, he didn't like that one bit. He grimaced and drove a nail into the door.

"Most people are going Christmas shopping. Lighting Advent candles. Giving time or money to charity." She studied the tree again, another ornament in hand.

"That's how *you* do it." Didn't take a genius to see how candy-sweet her holidays were. With songs about white Christmases and angels on high, good causes and candlelight services, she had the kind of life he'd forgotten about. Eight of the last nine Christmases he'd spent either on a forward post, a camp out in the middle of nowhere or gearing up for a deployment. Sometimes it got easy to forget the details of what he was fighting for and what he wanted his life to be after he laid down his rifle.

Maybe it was the picture of this life and not the woman that pulled at his heartstrings. Perhaps this glimpse of a dreamlike holiday would explain the well of emotion troubling him. He'd been jumping out of planes and fast-roping out of helicopters for most of his adult life. Sometimes a man wanted more.

And his gaze went right back to September. Sure enough, she was picture-perfect in a simple green sweater and jeans. He flipped off the switch, and the room fell into darkness. The flash and gleam of the jewel-colored twinkle lights shone like something off a Christmas card, adorning her with the sparkle of red, blue, yellow and green. With the colors burnishing September's hair and accenting her delicate profile, Hawk lost the argument with himself. He could try to logically explain away his soft spot for her with all kinds of reasons, but that didn't disguise the truth.

"The wreath looks great." She considered the ornament and moved it an inch to the left. The frail branch dipped down, swaying with the silvered ball. "Come help with the ornaments."

"I don't have the knack for it." That, and it would mean he would have to be near to her. Bad idea. "I'm a terrible ornament hanger."

"You did fine with the wreath." She had no idea how appealing she was, like a carol. She flipped a lock of hair behind her shoulder and chose another ball from the box. "I'll take my chances. Come help me."

His feet moved him forward and he learned something new. It was impossible for him to say no to her. Impossible to keep the walls up and the defenses strong.

"Don't know how much help I'll be." Gone were the days of his boyhood, where he was the one in charge of the tree. Of his little sister wanting decorations and his mother, lost to depression, having left them to make what Christmas they could. He chose a blue ball from one of the boxes, liking the sprinkles of glitter that formed the star of Bethlehem, and slid a hook through the eye. "Don't say I didn't warn you."

"Get over here, Gloomy Gus." Gloomy was the last thing she could possibly be, wreathed by the richly colored lights and twice as radiant. "That would look perfect right here."

Good thing he had control of his heart. He stalked toward her, the perimeter around his feelings reinforced. He shouldered close to her, teeth gritted, ignoring the wish tempting him. Easy to see how it would be for the guy who landed her as his wife, Christmas seasons just like this, each one better than the next. He hung the ornament where she'd indicated, and the glistening blue orb made the twig bow dangerously.

"It's not going to hold," he warned her.

"Sure it is. Have a little faith."

"Faith, sure, but this is a matter of physics." He was captivated by the mystery in her expression. He shifted away and pretended interest in choosing another ornament, but in truth, it was to study her more. He grabbed a hook just as the limb slumped, the ornament tumbled and bounced down the tree.

He caught it before it crashed to the floor. "See, Galileo was—"

"Yeah, yeah, I know who Galileo was." She batted him in the arm, a light playful slap.

His perimeter shattered, his defenses fractured. There was nothing left of his will. He could not hold back the rising tide of his adoration. He was not that strong.

"Next you will bring up something about Ptolemy and the stars." She took the holy star from him and hung it on a bough.

He was staring again. Way to go, Hawkins. He tried to act casual and reached into the storage bin. Maybe there would be something in here he could hang on the front porch and get some fresh air and his head clear.

"What's that?" She swept close, luminous with the blinking lights. When he didn't answer, she bent to take a look, squinting in the dark. "It's plastic mistletoe. It's a family tradition to hang a sprig over the front door. When we were little, Dad would chase us for a raspberry kiss every time he came home."

"I can picture it." He brushed a lock of hair from her face. It wasn't really in her way, but he took the excuse to touch her. To close the bridge between them. He caught her hand in his and lifted it over her head. He didn't know what made him do it. It just happened. His lips fit over hers in one tender brush—that just happened, too.

Chapter Seven

It was a perfect kiss. For an instant, September's eyes drifted shut and she let the sweetness sweep through her. It was something out of a dream. His mouth was patient and not demanding, and that made it easier to grasp his arm, hold on tight. Her mind stopped working. It took her a few long moments to realize this was no dream. Hawk was kissing her.

Kissing her! She broke away, watching the dance of light on his face. He seemed lost in a dream, too—the dream of Christmas, she told herself firmly. She uncurled her hand from his shirtsleeve and stepped away. The moment over, he bolted away, too, and together they stared at the mistletoe she held.

"Got to keep up the traditions." His glib remark told her that his hadn't been a serious kiss. "Want me to hang that for you?"

"Sure." She was shaken. Did it show in her voice? She couldn't tell. He looked pretty blasé as he scooped the plastic twig of mistletoe from her and ambled to the entryway. He scooted the ladder up and into place, quite as if their kiss hadn't happened.

She could not forget it. She fumbled with the hooks. They globbed together and she couldn't free a single one from the knot. When she did, two dozen of them tumbled to the floor.

"You okay over there?" His good-natured baritone held no hint as to what he was feeling.

"Just peachy." For a girl who didn't want to wake up from the dream. Who wouldn't have minded if the kiss lasted a few beats longer, because then she could have had time to absorb and process. To make sense out of why he had kissed her.

Get a grip, September. He kissed you. He didn't propose to you. She scooped up the last of the hooks, dumped them back into their original box and opened the next container of ornaments.

He didn't appear to be affected, but she was. Her hands continued to tremble, her knees stayed like jelly. Out of the corner of her eye, she watched him climb the ladder and drive a small white nail into the ceiling. She chose a hand-painted glass ball, careful not to drop it. She didn't trust her fingers. She didn't trust herself. All shields were down. How had Hawk gotten through her defenses?

"You were right." He startled her. Suddenly he came up behind her. "It's the perfect Christmas tree. You didn't need my help tonight, not really, but I'm glad to be here with you."

"You're a good friend." She wanted him to know she understood. It was only a friendly kiss. A holiday kiss. Nothing more. She wasn't one of those women who was prone to seeing romance everywhere—not anymore. "It wouldn't have been half so fun decorating this by myself, and I did need you. I could never have done the lights by myself."

"So you said, but your sister could have helped you." He reached out as if to brush her face, but his hand changed directions in midair and caught the length of her hair. He nudged it back behind her ear, although it hadn't been out of place.

Perhaps he felt more awkward than she'd guessed. That made two of them. Good thing she was a pro at covering up her true feelings. "You've packed up your toolbox."

"I can stay if you need me to, but your tree is nearly done. Unless there's anything else you want me to hang, fix or nail for you, I'd better be on my way." He didn't sound in a hurry to exit stage left.

Maybe she was reading too much into things. It was—she glanced at the wall clock—after nine. "You probably have an early day tomorrow."

"I'm picking up Pierce at Sea-Tac in the morning. We're driving to Canada." The only hint of tension was the tight line of his jaw. "We'll be gone for five days."

"You say that with such excitement, as if you're heading off on a Caribbean cruise." She hung another ornament, careful to keep her gaze on the tree. "Mountain glaciers have to be horribly cold this time of year. Are you staying at a lodge or a cabin or something?"

"A tent. We're roughing it."

"You'll freeze this time of year. Are you nuts?"

"Beyond a doubt." He laughed along with her. "This is fun for us. We get to test our mettle. We bundle up in goose down and build fire like cavemen. We eat beef jerky and complain about how cold we are. It's a blast."

"It certainly sounds appealing. Remind me to *never* go on a vacation with you."

"For you, I could make less challenging plans. I'm flexible." He hefted his toolbox, feeling as if he had not accomplished what he had set out to do, although he couldn't begin to explain what that was. Unsettled, wanting more and knowing he couldn't have it, he headed for the door. "When you head back to work, say hi to Comanche for me. I think he and I bonded."

"I'll be sure and mention you to him." She followed him to the door. "Want me to pick out a ride for you?"

"A ride? You mean, like a horse?" His hand lingered on the knob. One turn, and he would have to walk out the door. It was getting late, but did he want to go? No way.

"You agreed to go on the benefit ride. You promised, remember?" She could talk him into jumping to the moon, he figured.

"I'll be there." Probably not a good idea, because of his impulsive kiss. It stood between them right now. September wasn't as easygoing; there was something she held back just beneath the surface. She kept a few more paces between them than was necessary. When she smiled, her eyes didn't dance and sparkle.

Yep, the kiss was to blame. He opened the door, hooked one arm around the ladder and hauled it onto the porch. Rain speared under the porch roof, background music on a cold winter's eve.

"I'll call and leave the details on your answering machine." She hung in the doorway, probably not wanting to get wet or cold. Although it could be she was afraid he might plant another kiss on her.

Cool, Hawk. Real cool.

"You forgot your brownies. Let me go wrap them up for you—"

"No," he interrupted. "You keep 'em. I appreciate the meal. You're a good cook."

"You say that as if you were surprised."

"No. Maybe one day I'll cook for you."

"I would be brave enough to eat whatever you prepare."

"I'll hold you to it." His gaze slipped to her mouth. He couldn't help it. He thought of that kiss again, like peppermint and Christmas morning and a Sunday hymn all rolled together. "Good night, September."

"Good night, and thank you." She beamed

up at him, quiet and shy, a wholesome combination. "I appreciated your help tonight. I appreciate you."

"Back at you, cutie." Call him an idiot, but he apparently hadn't learned his lesson. He leaned down to slant his mouth over hers. One soft brush was all he allowed himself before he pulled away. He had only one explanation for his rash action. "Mistletoe."

"It's not directly over the door." She sounded amused, not really protesting at all.

"Close enough." He grabbed his tools and his ladder and hoofed it down the steps. "I'll call you when I get back."

"Be careful on that glacier."

"Count on it."

"Better yet, I'll pray on it." She waved her good hand in goodbye. Night had fallen, and as he left, Hawk was a shadow against the dark curtain of rain, so it made no sense why she could see him clearly. Maybe she wasn't looking as much with her eyes as with her heart.

The big, strapping man striding confidently through the storm was no longer a reminder from the past, Tim's Ranger buddy or a passing acquaintance. He was her friend, the man who had chased away her shadows and brought color and light back into her life. The tree lights blinked as if in perfect agreement as she closed the door against the damp, chilly night and moved to the window to watch his truck drive away.

Beside her the tree stood in silent reminder of the evening. She raised her hand to wave again, not sure if he could see her, as his pickup ambled down the road. Hawk, a faint silhouette behind the wheel, waved in return. The first stirrings of deep emotion fluttered to existence in her heart—hope in the darkness.

"Earth to Hawk."

As the freeway north of Seattle swished by beneath the hood of his truck, Hawk heard a distant amused voice. Shaking his head to clear it—not that it worked—he attempted to stay in the here and now. His mind was stuck in a loop that took him straight back to last night. Two kisses. Correction—two mistletoe kisses, and she didn't seem sorry about it. He shook his head again, hit his turn signal to pass and moved into the far left lane. "Sorry, buddy. I've got a lot on my mind."

"Apparently. Whenever I have that much on my mind, it always has to do with Lexie." His fiancée. Smirking, Pierce waited for affirmation. He already knew he was right.

Why deny it? Hawk maneuvered past the semi, keeping his eyes on the road. "I ran into September Stevens, Tim's—"

"I know who she is," Pierce interrupted, surprised. "She could barely speak to my family at the funeral. I've never seen anyone so devastated."

"I have." He thought of his mom. He knew about loss. He'd lost not only his dad in a logging accident, but his mother, too. "She's doing better. I was over at her place last night. She bought a nice little town house south of the city. I did a few repairs and hauled in her Christmas tree for her. No biggie."

Except for those kisses. He couldn't get rid of the feeling that he shouldn't have done that. September was off-limits. Any decent man would think so. She was still recovering from a deep heartbreak. She had once been his best friend's girl. He might have tried explaining those kisses away using the mistletoe, but the truth was he would have kissed her without it. It wasn't right to care about her in any other way than friendship.

"No biggie, huh?" Pierce, fearless on the

battlefield and smart tactically, was never easily fooled. "I understand, man. Don't sweat it. I've been there before. Fact is, I still am. Nearly killed me to leave Lexie behind. It doesn't get easier. Every time I go, it's leaving a piece of me."

"Hey, what kind of talk is that? This is your last outing as a free man." Not exactly your usual bachelor party. "Getting cold feet yet?"

"Not a chance, but Lexie keeps saying we should forget the expense and bother and head for Vegas. I know it's the stress of the preparations talking, but my mom would tan me for sure if she doesn't get a wedding. I'm the first of us to get married."

"I can see her really liking the wedding stuff."

"You're still going to be my best man, right?"

"*I* don't have cold feet." Although when it came to September, he should. Guilt tore through him. He couldn't bring himself to tell Pierce what had really happened last night. Maybe it was time to reevaluate this relationship with her. Since his normally impenetrable defenses and iron will had no effect around her, he ought to consider ending things.

"Take the next exit, would you?" Pierce gestured toward a freeway sign coming up on them pretty fast. "It's about chow time and I'm starving."

"Sure thing." Still troubled, Hawk tapped the turn signal and changed lanes just as the first drops of rain fell.

"I know you're getting antsy, handsome. You've been without a long ride for way too long." September gave the cinch a good tug and laid her casted hand against Comanche's stomach. "You aren't holding your breath, are you?"

Caught in the act, the palomino exhaled sheepishly.

"Every time," she told him. "That's how I know. You might as well not even try."

He shook his head, as if he had an opinion on that. He was the best horse in the entire world— okay, she was biased—but he tended to have a mind of his own. She buckled up, and they were ready to go.

"C'mon, boy." She caught his reins and led him down the aisle. "We can't take the trails up the mountain until they are all inspected. You don't mind, do you?"

Comanche lipped her ponytail, just glad to be with her. She knew, because that's how she felt. Grateful to be spending time with her best bud.

Her riding boots gave a satisfying knell alongside her gelding's steeled shoes as they followed the cement pathway past the riding arena.

"I didn't know you were cleared to ride." Colleen, her boss, appeared in the office doorway. "Did your doctor give you clearance?"

"Not only that, but I can come back to work whenever, if you'll have me." She dug in her jacket pocket and handed over the doctor's memo. "I'm not sure how useful I'll be in the barns, but I can do my lessons."

"Excellent. I'll put you in the office on Monday instead of cleaning stalls until that's healed." Colleen studied the paper and folded it in precise half. "I heard from Mrs. Toppins. She says Crystal is home and recovering nicely. The girl is already begging to resume her lessons."

"Sounds like Crystal." She had a definite soft spot for her favorite student. "I meant to call her mom today. I'm glad she isn't afraid to ride. A lot of kids wouldn't want to get back on a horse after an experience like that."

"She's got grit," Colleen agreed. "Speaking of which, I'm glad to see you here, too. I was worried."

"About me? Don't be. I've had my share of falls and I've gotten back up every time." The horse tugged on her ponytail again, and she stroked Comanche's nose. "About working in the office. You have to know I won't have the best typing speed with this cast."

"Speed isn't everything. I hear the phone ringing. Have a good ride."

"Thanks, Colleen." As her boss hurried into the office to catch the call, September led her horse the rest of the way to the trailhead. The way north—to the mountain—was barricaded, but there were others to choose from. She grabbed the saddle horn, slid her toe into the stirrup and lifted herself into the saddle. The gelding stood patiently, ears pricked and scenting the wind. Yep, he was glad to be headed out, too.

She reined Comanche to the right, choosing the meadow path that looped around the grounds. The cold wind ruffled his platinum mane, and the gathering gray clouds above suggested the weathermen would soon be right. Green grass spread like emeralds for a mile, broken only by the white board fencing where horses grazed and riders practiced their pace changes. Voices from the covered arena carried faintly. Grade-school-aged girls sat astride their mounts in the beginners' class in the far paddock, and their excitement reminded her of being a little girl on a much younger Comanche, living her dream.

She'd always felt that God had led her here. Years had slipped by, time passed by well spent with friends and riding and working hard for competitions. He had known her heart and brought her to this wonderful place where she had always been happy. Even in her darkest times after she lost her beloved Tim, this place was the best refuge for her hurting soul.

Comanche nickered at a nearby buddy, who looked up from grazing and whinnied back. They continued on at a leisurely walk. Good to be in the saddle again. She breathed in fresh country air. Robins and sparrows soared and chattered, hurrying to get their work done before the rain. Mount Rainier's beautiful glaciered peak was lost in a crown of clouds. Hawk. She wondered how he was doing, if he had reached the mountain whose glacier he intended to scale or if he was still on the road.

Her thoughts kept circling back to him. He'd been a true helper fixing the leak, and her foyer hadn't been so bright in a while. As for his kisses—

You don't have to think about them, she reminded herself as rain pinged off her hat. She lifted her face and let the droplets bathe her. Nice and relaxing after an unsettled day. Tension eased, as if washed away by the rain, and she realized how worked up she'd been over Hawk. And why? She drew in a cleansing breath. After the benefit ride, it wasn't as if she were going to see him again. Likely as not he would be deployed by the new year and she would have worried for nothing.

Comanche extended his neck, asking for more rein, commanding her attention. He wanted to run. Well, she was up for it. She signaled him with her knees and leaned into his gait change. He dug in with all fours, from a smooth trot to a rolling cantor. She felt stronger, as she always did, racing the wind with her best bud. Everything came clear. Hawk's kisses were nothing she needed to worry about. As lovely as they were, he wasn't dating her. He had to know love was the last thing she would ever risk again.

The ground raced by in a blur as Comanche broke into a fast gallop, and she left her troubles behind.

Talk about cold. Hawk drove the stake into the ground and checked the anchor rope's tension. It ought to hold in all but the highest winds. They had driven as far as they could and had barely enough daylight left to set up camp. They would ski in to the climb come morning. For now, dark had fallen and the rain had turned to snow.

"Got the fire going." Pierce came around the corner of the tent. "Want me to break out the hot dogs or the Spam?"

"Hot dogs." He hiked through the accumulating snow and dropped the hammer with the rest of the gear. "Any chance you got some water hot yet?"

"You're gettin' soft." Pierce shook his head. "You should have bailed out of the Rangers when you got the chance. Don't know how you are gonna make it two more years."

"Hey, *I'm* not about to be an old married man." Not that he blamed Pierce one bit. Married life sounded just fine with him. Which was odd. He liked being a lone wolf. Thinking about it made him think of September, and that couldn't be a good sign, so he grabbed his collapsible cup and a tea bag and hunkered down on a rock to check on the heating water.

"Tell me more about what happened after you carried her out of the mine shaft." Pierce broke open a package of beef franks and impaled a couple of them on a skewer before handing it over.

"There's nothing to tell. I checked on her at the hospital. I dropped by to help her out. Figured Tim would have wanted me to make sure she was okay." He took the skewer and held it over the lively flame.

"So you did it for Tim?" Pierce nodded with understanding. "I was always deployed, never got to know September very well, but I recall she was pretty and kind. Tim was crazy about her."

"I know." Guilt with pinpoint accuracy. A top sniper didn't have better aim. "Being crazy about her would be easy to do."

"Ah, I thought so." Pierce angled his meal over the cracking fire pit. "Tim would have expected her to go on with her life and find someone again. He would want a guy to take good care of her and treat her well. If you want my opinion, I think he would be glad if that man was you. Just something to think about."

Snow tapped on his parka and sizzled on the ring of rocks, and he gave his skewer a turn, watching the skins blacken as the meat cooked.

Pierce thought he was helping, but it hadn't removed the bullet of guilt lodged in his chest.

"Catch." Pierce tossed a hot dog bun over the fire and smoke.

Hawk caught it in one hand, caught a second one and pulled the skewer from the heat. Dinner was served.

The afternoon's light rain had turned into what sounded like a monsoon by the time September finished wiping down her kitchen counters. There. The chores were done for the evening. Satisfied, she hit the start button and the dishwasher chugged to life. The marble gleamed, the cabinets shone, the appliances sparkled in the white twinkle lights she had strung around the top edge of the upper cabinets.

The phone rang. Chessie, checking up on her. She didn't have to look at caller ID as she grabbed the cordless and turned off the overhead lights. She left behind the soft glow of the twinkle lights and headed to the living room. The gas fireplace was going, chasing the winter's chill from the room. "No, I don't have my feet up, but as soon as the phone rang I headed for the couch."

"How did you know it was me calling?"

"My big-sister radar beeped." She stretched out on the couch and grabbed the remote. "And no, I didn't overdo it at the stables. I needed to get in some saddle time before next week's event."

"Excuses. As if you need more time on the back of a horse." Beneath Chessie's tough-girl facade ran true caring. "You sound better. More like yourself."

"It takes more than a fall into a big hole in the earth to keep me down," she quipped, hit the mute button and began to channel-surf.

"You know I wasn't talking about that. You haven't sounded this chipper since…" She paused, as if she didn't want to cause any pain by bringing up Tim's name.

"I had a good day." That was the simplest explanation. She didn't know why she felt better—she certainly didn't want to pin that on one man. She was not that needy or fragile; she was the kind of woman who stood on her own two feet. "How did your day at work go?"

"The same old thing. Not much changes at the library. People check out books, they bring them back." Librarian humor. "Have you heard from Dad yet?"

They passed the next thirty minutes catching up on family news and holiday plans. In the background, September's thoughts were way too preoccupied with a certain new friend. After she said goodbye to her sister, she punched in Hawk's home number. His machine came on and his rugged baritone across the line made her smile. She left him the information he needed for the ride—just businesslike stuff. Nothing personal.

Except for the small detail that she was grinning ear to ear by the time she hung up. So what? She was looking forward to seeing the guy. They were friends. That was a prerequisite for a friendship, right?

Right, and so were those kisses. She rolled her eyes. Best not to think about the kisses.

Luckily, *Jeopardy* came on. One of her faves. She turned up the volume, calling out answers along with the contestants.

But what was at the back of her mind?

Yes. Hawk. He had taken up permanent residence in her thoughts.

Chapter Eight

The rain had miraculously cleared after it had been pouring for hours. It's a sign, September decided as she guided Comanche around the last corner and onto the main trail of the park. Clusters of trees waved, shedding the morning's rain with plops and plinks. A half dozen squirrels peeked out from branches and boughs to get a good look at all the activity. The local trail riders' association had a booth set up at the starting line, where she had volunteered last year.

People and horses were everywhere. She waited for a break in the line before dismounting, unwrapped General's reins from the saddle horn and led both horses to the booth.

"I'm glad to see you back in the saddle." A friendly face smiled up at her from behind a table. Fred Adkins made a check on his clipboard. "We were all so worried when you and that little girl went missing."

"Thanks for joining the search party." She opened a saddlebag. She had already sent a thank-you note to the association, for many of the members had volunteered. "It means a lot."

"That's what friends are for. Here are your T-shirts." He piled a small and an extra large on the table.

"And here is my donation." She traded six cans and two boxes of mac and cheese for the shirts. "And my sponsor sheet."

"You are phenomenal, as always. This is going to help feed a lot of hungry kids in our town." Fred straightened his shoulders, almost as if he were trying to get her to notice him. But did it work?

Not in the slightest. She grabbed the T-shirts, thanked him again and felt the back of her neck tingle. Comanche nickered in recognition. Hawk. He ambled toward her. In his black jacket, black jeans, black boots, he looked like the Special Forces soldier he was. His gaze found hers, and her soul stirred.

Why does he affect me so strongly, Lord? She would have loved to hear God's answer, because she didn't have a clue. The man had magnetism.

"I see you made it off the glacier okay." She handed him one of the T-shirts.

"No worse for the wear." He shrugged off his jacket and pulled the T-shirt over his head. "We had a great time. Challenged the ice. Roughed it like real men. Got in our bro bonding before his big day."

"When is his wedding?"

"Two days before Christmas." He caught the collar of her coat, helping her out of it.

Oh, his manner was so appealing. She tried to hide her giddiness as she pulled her new T-shirt on over the March of Dimes shirt she already wore. Both horses stood obediently, although Comanche was shaking his head up and down, as if trying desperately to say something.

"I think he's saying hi." She slid her arms into her coat sleeves, dangerously close to Hawk. He settled the garment at her shoulders. It was nice, how old-fashioned he was. "The black gelding who is politely waiting is General. He's one of the horses we rent out. Gentle as a lamb and very imposing."

"I came prepared." Surprising her, he hauled something out of his pocket. The horses nickered, excited by whatever he held in his hand.

"Peppermints." She laughed. Leave it to

Hawk to notice the details. "You saw me feed him one."

He nodded, and unwrapped two candies and offered one to each horse. Comanche dove for his. General politely lipped the treat from Hawk's palm.

"And one for you." He unwrapped a third candy and raised it to her lips.

Okay, she had never had a friend do this before, she thought as the peppermint melted on her tongue, but Hawk couldn't be anything more. They both knew it.

"Riders, welcome to our tenth annual Ride for Hunger." A voice aided by a bullhorn rose above the sounds of the milling crowd. September recognized the president of the riding club astride his handsome bay. "What a turnout. Thanks for being here. It might be a cold day, but we're a warm-hearted bunch. I'll see you at the finish line."

Cheers rose up from the crowd and the noise swelled as people mounted up. September couldn't resist sneaking a peek at Hawk. Through the president's little talk, he had been rubbing General's nose. The two struck an accord, and Hawk swiftly and competently adjusted the stirrup length.

"You thought I was new at this, huh?" He swung neatly into the saddle. "My grandma kept a pony at her place. When she was alive I would visit her quite a bit. I didn't get a lot of horse time in, I was more of a tree-climbing, fort-building kind of kid, but I know enough to keep my seat."

"You are one surprise after another." She should have known, she thought, rolling her eyes. She eased into Comanche's saddle and gathered her reins, unable to take her gaze off the man. Was there anything Hawk couldn't do?

"I strong-armed my Ranger buddies to contribute to the cause." With a wink, he pulled a half dozen checks from his pocket. "Do I turn them in now?"

"You can. Here, we'll take them over." She pressed her gelding into a slow walk. She hadn't realized most of the crowd had taken off, following the course through the park. Odd. How had she not noticed?

Fred, however, was still at the stand, glad to take the offered checks. His smile dimmed when he caught sight of Hawk and didn't try to flirt.

"So, this is what you do when you aren't at the stable?" Hawk asked, after waiting until they were on their way. "You ride for benefits. Hang out with other horse enthusiasts. Make donations to the food bank."

"Guilty. I've also been known to teach Sunday school."

"I should have known." His voice dipped low, amused. "I can see you leading a class. Little kids?"

"First and second graders. They are so funny and I always learn something new." She chuckled at something she didn't share with him. Maybe she thought he wouldn't be interested in kids. She would be wrong.

"Any other hobbies?" he asked.

"With what time? Only a true horseman would understand. Comanche is my hobby. He's my life, too." She leaned forward with a slight creak of the saddle to pat the palomino's neck. Comanche tossed his head and nickered, as if to say, *Of course. I deserve all her time.*

Hard to argue with that.

"What about you? Besides the ice-climbing thing, which is nuts in my opinion—"

"That's because you don't do it," he quipped, teasing her just to make her laugh. "A true mountaineer would understand."

"Hey, I didn't talk down to you when I said that."

"I know, but I couldn't resist." Laughter felt good, almost as great as being with her again. "There's nothing like being pitted against nature and winning. Besides, at the end of a climb when you are sitting on top of that mountain, sometimes pretty precariously, you can feel very close to God."

"That's what I like about you, Hawk. You can be funny, and you know how to be real, too." She beamed at him.

She liked him. She said the word *like*. He sat straighter in the saddle, feeling mighty good. She had stayed on his mind through the last handful of days on the side of the mountain and throughout the return trip home. The guilt dogging him hadn't faded one whit, but something began to outshine it—the strength of his feelings for her.

"You have to be real when you do what I do for a living." It was that simple. "You become the job. It's something you love and feel commitment for. But you know all that. If I could have hobbies, aside from skiing and climbing, I would like to do a lot of things."

"You are one of those guys with a long list of

things he wants to accomplish before he dies, right?"

"How did you know about the list?" He hadn't told anyone about his goals in life—except for God.

"Good guess."

The air had turned damp, the way it did before a good rain. He breathed in fresh air, scenting the nearby sound. He could hear the lap of the waves against the rocky shore between the *clomp, clomp* of the horse's hooves.

"So, what's at the top of your list?"

"That's awfully personal, isn't it?" He wanted to keep it casual, safely away from the crater in his heart. The one that she was bound to notice and fault him for. The Lord knew it had always been his Achilles' heel, the reason he might always be alone.

"Hey, we're friends. We are supposed to be personal."

Hard not to look at her, cute and expecting something from him, and not give it to her. He bit the bullet and admitted the truth. Easier to stare off at the blue-gray sound ebbing against the gravel beach than to let her see his vulnerability. "A family. That's at the top of my list."

She didn't say anything for a moment. He'd

surprised her. Sure, that would surprise every-one. He cleared his throat. Since he had gone this far, he might as well say it all. "The free spirit thing is because it's easier. I don't want to make commitments."

"Being Special Forces comes with a cost." Her soft alto deepened with understanding. She had paid a price, too. They rode in silence for a moment, taking advantage of the calm of the water. The first drops pattered on the gray rock and the trail ahead of them. The low gray sky turned the sound pewter-gray, and the quiet rev-erence of the land and water felt as if God had sent the peaceful moment just for the two of them. A healing balm of sorts, to ease the mem-ory of war and loss, of two futures without love.

"How many kids do you want?" she asked after a long while.

"I'd like at least two or three, but that wouldn't depend entirely on me." His future wife, who-ever she might be, had always been an idea, a wish unformed. Maybe because he was never certain he could let any woman close enough to want to stick with him. Now, as the path ahead turned away from the water to cut through the greenbelt of the park, he saw September's face—his future. "I've always wanted enough kids so that we feel like a family, but not too many so that I'm outgunned."

"You want a nice balance. Understandable."

"I want what I didn't have growing up. I'm lucky I had next-door neighbors who included me. I was almost a part of the family, I was over at their house so much. It got so that Mrs. Granger would set a place for me at the table without even asking if I wanted to stay. It was just assumed."

"I'm glad you had them. How old were you when you lost your dad?"

"Eight." The suddenness had been the hardest part. One morning, life was normal. A happy mom, a caring dad and he was a content kid off to catch the school bus. By day's end, that life was gone for good. Not something he wanted to talk about. That wasn't why he'd come back. That wasn't why he'd been dying to see her. He swiped rain from his eyes. "How about you?"

"Me? No, I don't want kids." She tensed, shifting away from him.

"You don't want kids? That can't be." The words were out before he could think them through. The moment he heard what he had said, he would have given anything to be able to turn back time and keep the thought to himself.

"Of course I want kids, except I'll never get married." She tried to fake a smile, but there was no hiding her sadness. He could feel it on the air and in his soul.

"Maybe one day?" He gave General a little heel so he would catch up to Comanche. September didn't turn toward him. Her hair tumbled like a curtain, shielding her from his sight. Her silence hurt, and he felt his hopes slipping. "Down the road, I mean. There might come a day in the far future when you find you can love again."

"I won't do it." She sounded so sure—sad and sure, all at once. "Never again."

His heart cracked right open in two equal parts, leaving him vulnerable and defenseless. He didn't know what to say, so he stayed quiet. The rocking gait of the horse, the other riders up ahead, the trees singing in the rain, even the chilly damp were all memorable. A glorious day, sure, but it turned out to be one of his darkest.

"I'm impressed." September gave Comanche a final rub with the towel—he was fresh, dry, warm and clean—and took a similar towel Hawk was offering her. "Not many guys would volunteer to help with the horses. You did a great job, too."

"I even did a decent job with the hoof pick cleaner thing."

She laughed; she couldn't help it. Happiness bubbled out of her. She gave the towels a toss into the laundry barrel and took hold of Comanche's lead. "This way, cowboy. All we have left to do is to stable them, and we're done."

"Great. I'm starving."

"You are always starving." As the stops for ice cream, a hot dog and, less than an hour ago, an enormous pretzel at a kiosk near the benefit's booth attested. "I would hate to see your food budget."

"Daunting."

The man could make her laugh. She led the way down the main aisle. It was quiet this late in the day, the lessons done. Only the die-hard riders, considering the sounds of horse hooves coming from the arena. It had been forever since she'd been this happy. The day felt light, the world around her hopeful and her spirit brightening. Hawk's friendship was turning out to be a true blessing.

"Come home with me and I'll feed you." She opened General's gate. "It's the least I can do for making you ride for hours in the rain."

"The pouring rain," he corrected, leading the black gelding into his stall. "I'm wet to the skin. You might owe me two dinners. Better yet, maybe I should treat you."

"What do you have in mind?"

"You're worried, right?"

"Just a tad. More like curious."

"Nope, I'm not going to tell you. You will have to stay in suspense." General dove into his feed trough. Hawk unclipped the lead and closed the gate. "Fine. I'll give you one hint. Noodles."

"That isn't a help. A lot of foods have pasta in them."

"True." Trouble danced in his eyes. Definitely a man she was going to have to keep an eye on. He was too charming for his own good. She spoke to Comanche and led him two stalls down. "I could go for carbs."

"Awesome. We are in perfect accord."

"We are." And it felt wonderful. The early conversation hadn't been forgotten—how could it be? Her great sadness about never loving again meant no children, no family of her own, which was a great weight she could not ignore. But Hawk didn't press her or try to talk her out of her decision, as everyone else had done.

No, instead of pointing out that she could adopt, or go into foster care or that ten years from now, or even twenty, she could change her mind, Hawk had offered unspoken understanding and spent the rest of the day making her laugh.

Just as he was doing now. Noodles. Really. What kind of hint was that? There was an Italian restaurant not far away, on the main road. She could go for lasagna, not that she needed the calories.

He held the passenger door for her—since he had commandeered her keys and her pickup. The trailer was already unhitched, cleaned and stowed, which meant they were free to go and indulge in noodles.

"How long has it been since this truck has had any work done on it?" He settled behind the wheel and turned the key.

"The last time I could afford it." She could tease, too. "I had an appointment, which I had to cancel because I was in the hospital."

"Ah, that would explain things." It took a few

tries for the starter to catch. "You could use a new clutch, too."

"It's on my list. I keep lists, too." She reached for her seat belt, but he was quick enough to take the buckle from her and fasten it. Thoughtful, since it was harder to do with her hand in a cast.

"I am well aware of your list, beautiful." He put the truck in gear and pulled into the gravel drive. Rain smeared the windshield faster than the wipers could keep up, but he drove with confidence and, apparently, eagle-eye vision. "You are keeping track of my faults. Have you made any additions?"

"Fearless driving. That's a flaw. There could be a cow in the road and you would never see it."

"I would see it." He oozed far too much confidence, but she believed him. Nor did he seem troubled by her comment. "What else?"

"You've become a good friend."

"That's a fault?"

"Well, there's a downside. You will be heading back to places unknown, like Afghanistan." She focused on the heater vent and adjusted it, although she clearly was looking for a distraction. "And then you will be an occasional e-mail, maybe a phone call now and then."

"I always come back. We can hang when I'm in town, right?"

"Sure."

"But it's not the same." He got that—he understood a lot. Traffic was heavy and he waited at the crossroads. He wouldn't lie to himself. He was falling for her. He could try to fight with himself over it; he had more self-discipline than most. But he also knew he wasn't in control of this. These feelings were bigger and greater than anything he'd known before. There was no way to stop them.

"We can still spend time together, right?" He tossed that out after pulling into a lane of traffic.

"Sure. You probably go to a church near the post, but do you want to join me tomorrow?"

"Just try and stop me." He signaled and pulled into a puddled driveway. The modest establishment's sign flashed cheerfully in the fading daylight. "What do you think?"

"This is a Thai place."

"Right."

"Noodles." She laughed. Again. Yep, life was

definitely better with Hawk around. Being with him made her world right.

Even when he was laughing, he was breaking inside. Through a shared meal and lively conversation, he stayed friendly and upbeat on the outside, but all he could think about was her confession she would never marry.

Never was a big word. One that devastated him. He refused to let her know it as he paid the bill, walked her to the truck and helped her in. The rain had paused, with dampness like vapor in the air and the black clouds above promising another shower.

This was a one-way street, he realized as he pulled out of the lot. She sat beside him, backlit by streetlights, regaling a tale of a stubborn show pony, a little girl and a huge mud puddle in one of the riding fields. September glowed— there was no other word for it. Her humor, her personality, her being dazzled him.

"Comanche shook his head through it all, as if he couldn't believe what he was seeing." Her laughter rang gently. "The pony wouldn't stop rolling. Little Hailey was covered in mud and crying—she got her new pink outfit dirty— and I comforted her while trying to get this pony to get up, which he wouldn't. It started to rain. It took three other people and two hours to get him back on his stubborn feet. I was still finding mud—under my fingernails, inside my boots—the next day."

She probably had no idea how adorable she was. How she had him all but wrapped about her little finger. She had no notion he was falling hard and fast or how much being with her hurt him. It didn't take much to see a future with her—one just like this. With her bright and lively, charming him evermore with one stable tale or horse adventure after another. Always, he would be enthralled. That future could not be. She did not want to walk down that path with him. No, she preferred to be alone.

Lord, please send me a sign. What should I do? He pulled into the park's lot and parked next to his truck. "I had fun today."

"And helped a good cause." Her hair had dried in the restaurant, into soft waves from the humidity. The spice-colored locks framed her face and made her look enchanting—someone far too whimsical and sweet to be real.

"Let me help." He unsnapped her buckle for her.

"You are always doing that, always helping

me." She studied him with appreciation—a beautiful sight for him to see. At least he knew she cared. Not the way he needed her to and not anything like how he cared for her, but he would take it.

"I'm the kind of friend you can depend on." Nearly killed him to say the word *friend,* but he meant the rest of it. He would always be there for her, come what may. Beyond duty, beyond devotion, even if she would never love him.

"I'll remind you of that come the next fundraiser." She didn't have a clue what he had meant or an inkling of what he felt.

That was all right. All that mattered was that she looked more like the woman he remembered, full of life and peaceful joy. When he handed over her truck and helped her behind the wheel, he didn't see anything more than friendship in her manner. It stung, but he knew she was giving him all she could. She thanked him again, gave him directions to the church and waved before she put the truck in gear and drove off.

She really had no idea. He watched her truck amble through the lot and hesitate on the main road. She turned left, toward home, taking his heart with her.

The rain returned as gently as if heaven had sent it. The future he saw with September was a wish that could not come true. Alone, battling defeat, he unlocked his truck and hopped behind the wheel. In some ways, it had been a tough day. He feared tomorrow having to be her friend—and nothing more—would be tougher.

Chapter Nine

The sanctuary buzzed with conversations and excitement in the moments before the organist started to play. September loved the old-fashioned church with its intricate carvings and plentiful cathedral-style stained-glass windows. Soft daylight made the colors glow as if divinely touched.

"You're looking chipper." Chessie barreled down the row from the left-hand aisle and dropped into the pew beside her. She clutched the program and her big handbag. "How many times have I told you? You put in too many hours at the stables. A little downtime has done you a world of good."

"I do feel more rested." While being off work went against her grain, she liked staying busy and keeping active. But her big sister had a point. She had poured herself into her work and stayed at the stables long after her work hours were over because that had freed her from having to face her grief. Going home knowing there would be no letter or e-mail waiting for her, or no chance Tim would call, had been too hard. It had been easier to stay occupied.

"I hope you have the good sense not to go back to work too soon." Chessie, with evidence to support her argument, forged ahead. "You should stay home until the doctor takes your cast off."

"I'm going back tomorrow."

"To riding?" Chessie frowned. "You can't do that. What about your arm?"

"I don't ride with my arm. Besides, I did just fine on the benefit ride. Which reminds me. You owe me a check to the town's food bank." She almost laughed when her sister's frown deepened. "Relax. I'm working in the office. You don't have to get so worked up."

"I'm your sister. It's my job." Chessie tucked her program aside, opened her purse and withdrew her wallet. Instead of writing a check, she stopped to glance around.

"Looking for someone?" It was so unlike Chessie, she had to ask.

"Not really." She released the pen neatly tucked into her checkbook and uncapped it. Something had changed, though. September tried to figure out where her sister had been gazing—toward the front, where a knot of people were talking at the head of the aisle. One of them was a rather handsome man in a navy suit and tie. "Were you looking at that guy?"

"Me? Don't be silly. I don't look at men. That would be too forward." Chessie's tone held just enough shock that it could have been trying to cover up something else, like vulnerability, maybe embarrassment.

"He looks familiar. Who is he?" Curious now, she couldn't let it drop. The organ finished the last refrain and started the first notes of "Amazing Grace."

"He used to live down the street from us. Jon Matthews. You might not remember him. He's back in town now. He took a job at a law firm in downtown Tacoma." Chessie sounded casual as she tore off the check and handed it over. "He saw me in the parking lot and asked me to go with him to the church's New Year's Eve dinner."

"Did you accept?"

"I told him I would think about it. I haven't

seen him since his family moved away in high school, which means I hardly know him. He could have terrible habits and dreadful faults for all I know." Chessie was hiding something.

Maybe a schoolgirl crush? Was she nursing affection for this man after so many years? September folded the check in half and slipped it into her purse. Her sister might be abrupt and forceful, but she had a tender heart. Her intentions were always the best. "Maybe you should say yes."

"This, coming from you?" Chessie nearly dropped her pen. She tucked it back into the little holder inside her checkbook and zipped her purse. "The last time we had this discussion, oh, a month ago, you told me to avoid romance. It always lets a girl down."

"Well, we are both children of divorce," she pointed out, maybe a little defensively because she had a feeling where her sis was going with this. "We are more realistic than most."

"Sure, that must be it. So, why should I say yes? He might be one of those men who are controlling after they marry you. Maybe he has a gambling habit."

"I see that smirk. Maybe he's a nice guy who would appreciate some good company for a Friday meal. How about that?" She squeezed her sister's hand. "I think you should go. He was a hunk in high school, and a kind guy. I'm sure he still is."

"Okay. I will." Chessie smiled, but it was short-lived. The church was more crowded, the pews mostly full, so it was simple to spot the brawny-shouldered man hiking up the right-hand aisle.

"Hawk." Happiness swept through September, a pure streak of joy that, like a sudden flash of sunlight after being in the dark, felt almost too intense to bear. She tried to dial it down, reining in her emotions as she patted the space beside her. "Is that you? I hardly recognize you."

"It's been awhile since I've put on a shirt and tie. The post's chapel is more casual." He slipped into the row and dropped next to her. "You are lovely."

"It's just a dress." She flushed, unable to explain why his compliment affected her or why she was glad he thought she looked nice. "You remember my sister, of course."

"Hi, Chessie." He offered her his most charming smile, probably thinking that he would warm his sister's icy stare.

He would be wrong. Before September could

say more the organ stilled, and their minister appeared, friendly and wise as always.

"Good morning, friends," he greeted the congregation warmly.

"You and I have to talk," Chessie whispered in her ear, and gave Hawk a pointed look.

Poor Hawk. He had to have caught it, but he remained respectfully unaware as he turned toward the altar. She wanted to say something reassuring to him and let him know how glad she was to see him again, but the minister called out to stand and join hands.

When Hawk's fingers caught hers and helped her to her feet, something happened. Life trickled into her wounded spirit like dawn after a bleak winter storm, like a promise of peace to come, of laughter and hope. He was doing this to her, drawing her out of the dark, helping her to feel.

Years ago, she and Hawk had been little more than acquaintances. Who would have guessed that the different roads they both walked would bring them here? It seemed like God's doing. She had been certain all her prayers went unanswered, but standing at Hawk's side in the sanctuary filled with light and reverence, she saw that God had been walking with her all along.

She hadn't been able to feel it, but that didn't mean that God wasn't there. He was showing her that Tim's loss hadn't taken her heart. She could feel it beating again.

Thankful, she bowed her head and listened to the minister's voice lift in prayer.

"I'm glad to see that gutter is holding up." Hawk paused on the front step to inspect the work he'd done. "Wouldn't want you to get mad at me for shoddy workmanship."

"You? Shoddy? Not a chance."

She stood in the doorway, beautiful even in the T-shirt and faded jeans she had changed into. He'd thought her amazing in the simple blue dress she'd worn, but he preferred this side of her—wholesome girl-next-door sweetness.

"I have to apologize for my sister," she went on to say. "She isn't happy about our friendship the way I am."

"I'm not out to break your heart."

"Oh, I know." She waved his concern away, as if she had no idea there was a deeper meaning to his comment. "She knows what I went through. She doesn't want me to hurt like that again."

"Neither do I." He understood what Chessie

meant. He had been there, too. Twice—as a kid growing up, and the first time he'd spotted September on that dark mountain. No way could he tell her that Chessie was right on target. The older sister had been able to see what the younger could not. As hard as he tried to hide his affection, it had to show. When he smiled at her, his defenses were down, his soul on display.

He stepped inside, toolbox in hand. The mistletoe hung overhead like a beacon flashing, Remember the Kisses. As if he could possibly forget. That had been a special moment for him, but what had it been for September? The way she blushed and hurried by him suggested she remembered, too, and she wasn't eager for kiss number three.

He followed her into the kitchen. He'd been pretty devastated yesterday, up some of the night feeling too frustrated to sleep. But in church this morning her face had brightened when she'd spied him in the aisle. He had to wonder. Was he entirely alone in his affections? Was there a chance her feelings could change?

"I made you a sandwich in case you didn't grab lunch at your apartment." She opened the refrigerator. "There's soda, butterscotch pudding, leftover Thai food from last night."

He resisted the urge to pull her into his arms. He wanted to know what it would be like to hold her against his chest, she who was so very dear to him. He shook his head. "Later. I want to get going in the garage. What do you usually do on a Sunday afternoon?"

"After I've changed out of my church clothes, you mean?" She closed the fridge and leaned against it. She'd drawn her hair back into a ponytail, leaving wispy curls to tumble around her face and emphasizing the delicate cut of her high cheekbones. "You know what I do. I spend time with Comanche. I realize you don't have a lot of free time. So why are you doing this? You need to have some fun while you can."

"Tinkering with cars is fun."

She frowned at him playfully, as if she refused to believe him. "When is your next deployment?"

"Mid-January." He pushed open what had to be the garage door—sure enough, it was—and searched for the light switch. The last thing he wanted to see was the look on her face. "I'll be gone for six months. It's a limited thing, we think. I'll be back sometime in June."

"So in other words, you are spending one

of your last weekend afternoons replacing my truck's starter?"

"Like I said. Fun." Light tumbled down on her pickup and her otherwise empty garage. This was, like everything, neat as a pin. That appealed to the Ranger in him. He set down the heavy box. "I'll be perfectly happy. If you trust me to stay here alone, why don't you head over to the stables? Give Comanche a howdy from me."

"Oh, I cannot abandon you here. That's not right—"

"It is, if I say so." He drew his keys from his pocket and pressed them into her hand. He was getting used to the sweep of affection that hit him like an undertow every time he was around her. "Take my truck. Go ahead."

"I'm supposed to play while you work?"

"Like I said. Fun. Besides, won't Comanche be expecting you?" Overwhelmed by a richer tone of caring, he brushed back a silken curl from her face. Surprise flashed across her features, whether from his touch or his words, he didn't know. "You don't want to let him down."

"No, but I don't want to let you down, either."

That mattered to him. A lot. Maybe she cared more than he'd thought, more than she realized.

"I'll be happier knowing you are doing what makes you happiest. Go on, get outta here. I want you to."

She couldn't miss the tenderness in his tone. He probably should have tried harder to hide it, but that wasn't his forte. He couldn't be sure, but she looked a little dazed as she nodded, his keys in hand.

"I'll be back later, then." She retreated, walking backward through the kitchen. "I'll have my cell on me, so call if you need to."

"Sure thing." He fought images threatening to take over his brain—glimpses of a future with her hurrying off to the stables to ride or work. With him working on the trucks or on a honey-do list around the town house. Maybe even getting a horse of his own so they could spend Sunday afternoons riding the mountain foothills.

I want it so much, Lord. Is it possible? Or am I chasing after a dream I can't have? The front door opened and closed. A few moments later his truck started outside on the driveway and powered away.

He popped the hood and got right to work sorting through the tools and getting out the ones he would need. He had to consider September's side of things. She wasn't ready to let anyone close, much less open her heart. Sure, he understood that. He was guilty of the same thing himself. It was why he'd spent most of his adult life alone, and his few girlfriends hadn't been around for long. He blamed his job, and that was part of it. It was tough to build a relationship when you were almost always apart and with half the globe separating you. But he had been at fault, too. He'd never let anyone close, not as he'd let September.

He'd opened himself up, and it had to be to the one woman who couldn't do the same. He grabbed the droplight and hung it on the upraised hood. He uncoiled the power cord as he went, and knelt in front of the outlet. September had shut herself down to survive—surviving was something he knew about. In the heat of battle when a mission went south, you focused on shoring up your defenses, protecting your six and getting your men out alive. Losing wasn't an option, so that meant that you fought with all you had.

He figured that was how September did it. She had gotten this far in survival mode, but that was only good for so long. When the battle was over, when the turmoil was past, you had to deal and figure out a way to move on with what you learned along the way. He grabbed the drop cloth and gave it a shake to unfold it. He had learned long ago that it was his choices that defined a man, and what he fought for and stood for every step of the way.

He spread the cloth over the polished fender and chrome-accented grille. Remembering the change that widened September's expressive eyes when he'd taken her hand, he had to believe there was a possibility. Maybe a small one, maybe bigger, he didn't know. He had to let her know how he felt. Life was too short to waste the chance for something great.

"I should have known." Chessie strode out of the main aisle, dressed to ride. "You couldn't stay away, could you?"

"No lectures, please." She had enough on her mind without trying to convince her sister that she wasn't going to break into pieces. "Did you just get here, or are you finishing up?"

"I've got Princess saddled for the arena, but we haven't started yet. It's pretty crowded." Chessie didn't seem too concerned about it. "We could take a trail ride, if you want. They opened the lower trail, so it's safe."

"That's a relief. I'm glad to know that won't

happen to anyone again." She stopped by her cubicle, set up in one of the forward stalls. Her desk was tidy, although a huge stack of mail and another of messages had built up. "I need to call Mrs. Toppins and check on Crystal today. Make sure she's still getting better."

"I'm surprised you aren't spending the afternoon with that Hawkins guy."

"There's plenty of the afternoon left for that." She knew a comment like that would drive her sister nuts, and so she smiled as she flipped through the address file on her desk. She found the Toppins' card with their home info and slipped it into her jean pocket. She would call from home later. "How did it go with Jon Matthews?"

"And that's your business, why?" Chessie didn't sound as harsh as usual, although she was sure trying to.

September wasn't fooled. "Because you're my sister, as you are so fond of telling me."

"That much is true." She ambled up to the desk and took Tim's picture from the hutch shelf. "I'm going to the dinner with him. It's been awhile since I've had a date."

"That's because you try to keep everyone at a comfortable distance." September sidled up to look at Tim's picture, too. Even years later it continued to hurt to see what she had lost, but not as much, she realized. She could study Tim in his army dress uniform without feeling as if she were crumbling into pieces. When he had died, much of her had died, too. So much that it didn't seem possible that she would go on living.

His dark hair, his kind brown eyes, his dependable presence pulled at her, true, but not in the same way. She thought of all the good times they'd had together—bowling, because he had been so fond of it, going on church outings, picnics in the rain. Those memories were delightfully hazy, like something good out of her past, images she would always smile over.

But images she no longer pined for. Times she had loved, but were gone now. That future was forever gone, but she could go on living. She understood that now. She began to realize how lost she'd become and how much of her had died with Tim. Sadness filled her. She still loved him, except that love had inexplicably changed. It had grown like the memories—dear and forever sweet, but no longer possible.

She could not spend the rest of the days the Lord had given her living for the past.

September set the picture on the shelf and let go. "I'm glad you agreed to go out with Jon."

"Me, too." Chessie led the way to the aisle, waving to a few fellow riders as they passed by. "Since we've talked about my love life, it's only fair we talk about yours."

"*Mine?* I don't have a love life." What on earth could her sister be talking about? She whipped down the aisle, vaguely realizing she was moving faster than usual. "Don't tell me you want me to start dating again?"

"I thought you already were."

Had Chessie lost her mind? Comanche nickered a welcome and pressed his nose into her hands. She took a moment to greet him, wondering what her sister could possibly be thinking. Then it struck her. "I'm not dating Hawk."

"Aren't you?"

"This is me you're talking to. Me." She couldn't imagine anything so preposterous. Her pulse thundered so hard, it was like thunder in her ears. "We are friends. Trust me, there's nothing romantic going on."

"Fine, okay, no need to get so defensive. That's *my* personality defect." Chessie crossed her arms over her chest. "I was just asking, that's all."

"You have to know Hawk and I can't be more than friends." Since Comanche was teething her zipper, she helped him out and unwrapped a couple of the candies from the peppermint supply she always kept in her coat pocket. "It's totally casual."

"Fine. I believe you."

I wish I did, September thought as she watched Comanche crunch happily on his treats. Something had happened in the house today when Hawk had given her his keys, some indefinable spark of emotion that made her see him not as a friend, but as a man. A wonderful and charming man who had rescued her from her sorrow as surely as he had carried her out of the mine shaft.

You cannot care about Hawk, she ordered herself as she led Comanche down the aisle. *You must not care for him like that.*

Colleen strolled into the tack room, changing the track of the conversation. After a brief chat and saddling up, she and Chessie hit the trail. The mountainside smelled crisp from the cold and the pine scent of the forest was a perfect complement to the time of year. With Christmas a little more than a week away, she and Chessie tossed around ideas on gifts for Dad and Estelle, their stepmom, who was especially hard to shop for. They talked about last-minute gifts and donations to the church's charity tree.

September couldn't remember the last time the foothills had looked so beautiful. The crystal-blue sky stretched from emerald mountainsides to the sparkling blue-gray water of the Puget Sound, and the sun shone with a brilliance she hadn't seen in years. By the time their ride was over, the temperature had fallen and the winds had risen. Shivering, they hurried their horses into the barns and talked while they rubbed them down, stabled them and headed back to their vehicles.

Chessie raised an eyebrow at Hawk's truck. "I'm only going to say this once, and then I'll leave it be."

"I know you, sister dear. That's impossible." Since she knew what was coming, she wanted to keep it light, so she hit the remote, which unlocked the doors, and tossed Chessie a troublesome grin.

"No, it isn't, and do you know why?" She unlocked her sensible conservative beige sedan. "Because you are like your old self again. I have my sister back. But what I have to say is for your own good."

"It always is." She couldn't help it. She wrapped Chessie in a big hug, because she loved her. No one could ask for a better champion or a better sister. "You don't have to worry about me anymore."

"That won't stop me." She was smiling as she opened her car door. "Hawk isn't just a soldier, he's a Ranger. He does dangerous things in dangerous places all over the world. Just like Tim did."

"I know."

Chessie's words stayed with her on the short drive home, a warning she could not ignore. Just as she could not ignore the comforting warmth of his friendship, the way she could depend on him and how alive she felt because of him. Maybe it was simply the basic connection to another person, something she had been avoiding for too long, that had done that. Maybe that was why he was a balm to her wounds—she didn't know—but she was glad Hawk was in her world. Very glad.

She parked the truck in her driveway, shut off the lights and locked the doors. Sunset was settling in to the western sky, brushing bold streaks of violet and rose, and burnishing treetops with a heavenly golden glow.

"Welcome home." Hawk appeared on the front step, a welcoming friend, a cherished buddy and more. "Perfect timing. I just took dinner out of the oven."

"Dinner? Did you warm up the Thai leftovers?"

"Not a chance, gorgeous. I made my famous tuna and noodle casserole just for you." He strolled closer, bringing the sunset with him.

A connection bound them, she couldn't deny it. Her spirit brightened and her world came into perfect focus all because he took her hand.

Chapter Ten

"Hawk, I can't believe you did all this."

The joy layering her voice was all the reward he needed. He'd worked the entire afternoon, first in her garage and then her kitchen. He wanted her to know the man he was. He was glad he'd taken the time to set the table with the china he'd found in the upper cabinets and candles standing in crystal holders. He shrugged. "It's nothing fancy, but I thought it might hit the spot."

"It smells amazing." She took off her coat, and he was there to help her with it. The floral scent of her hair, the winter wind on her clothes, the healthy glow to her cheeks made him want to memorize the moment. If only he could slow down time and make this evening last forever.

"Where did you learn to cook like that?" She

took the coat from him and hung it over the back of one of the breakfast bar chairs.

"My mom." He took matches out of his pocket and broke one from the book. "She was a firm believer a boy should know his way around the kitchen."

"Smart woman." September nodded approvingly, and he didn't miss the appreciation in her gaze.

"She is a chef." He struck the match and touched the flame to the first taper. "I was one lucky kid. Mac and cheese took on a whole new meaning at my house. I'll have to make that for you, too, sometime. The best on the planet."

"I won't argue."

"Good. Then it's a date." Why that word popped out, he couldn't say. Probably his subconscious at work, already well aware of what his conscious mind wasn't quite ready to admit, even to himself. The candles lit, he shook out the match and set it in the sink. "I ought to have you over to my place, maybe after Christmas. I'll do the works. A fancy salad, garlic bread and some sparkling grape juice."

"I'll bring dessert. I make a pretty good chocolate cheesecake."

"Great. We could do it for New Year's Eve, unless you have plans."

"Not me. Chessie was going to drag me over to her house, but now she's going out with this guy she's had a crush on forever." She was talking a little fast as he pulled out a chair at the table for her. "So that leaves me free."

"Good for her. Good for us." He helped her scoot in her chair, trying hard to sound casual. She needed that security, he understood. She wasn't ready for serious yet. For a Ranger trained to successfully face, execute and complete every mission, he was out of his depth. His training did no good. There wasn't a force strong enough on this earth to stop the tides of his heart. He had no defense against it. He could only do his best to be what she needed— a friend and nothing more. He circled around to his chair and dropped into it. "I'll rent a movie and we can make a real evening of it."

"Perfect, since we both would be home alone otherwise." She draped the cloth napkin over her lap, dainty as could be. "Part of the mountain trails are open again. It's safe."

"Funny, it's been so long ago that this area was mined for silver. Everyone's forgotten those old days. You have to wonder how many mine heads were covered over with boards, and time and the forest did the rest." He held out his hands, thinking that time changed all things. Looking at the amazing woman across the table, he had to wish that her decision never to love again might be left behind and forgotten, too. "Do you want to say the blessing, or should I?"

"Are you kidding? You *are* the guest and the cook."

Was it his imagination, or did her fingers tighten on his? Was the warmth in her voice of a deeper tone? Profound tenderness welled up within him, refreshing to a part of him that he didn't know was wrung out and worn. With hope, he bowed his head in prayer. "Dear Lord, thank You for these blessings we are about to receive and for strengthening our friendship. Please guide us in being your helpful servants in all ways, amen."

"Amen."

He liked the way her sincere alto blended with his voice. He adored the reverent way she bobbed her head, a little end to her praying, and flashed him a megawatt smile. Full of life and dazzlingly wholesome. Not the September he remembered from long ago or the sad woman who had lost her true love, but a new woman, more beautiful than she had been before.

"How was your ride?" Since he'd been the cook, he grabbed her plate and dished up a serving of casserole. He did his best to keep it casual. "At least it didn't rain for you."

"Unlike yesterday when we were riding." She sparkled with amusement as she took the plate he offered. "Chessie was there."

"I didn't know your sister still rode." He scooped up a helping for himself.

"Oh, she loves to ride, she just stopped being horse crazy in her teens. Something I have never successfully been able to do." She spooned out a few pieces of buttered carrots and asparagus, lifted the vegetable bowl and passed it to him. "Otherwise I would have gone to college and become a librarian like my sister."

"You, a librarian? I can't see it. That would put you indoors all day." He dished up a heap of vegetables. "Although I'm sure you would make a fantastic one, if that's what you decided you wanted."

"I can't see myself boxed in all day. I love working with horses and with kids. Even the barn work puts me in a good mood. The horses always do something funny, even Mel."

"Who's Mel?"

"He's this incredibly obstinate horse. He belongs to the stable. Colleen, my boss, heard from the vet about this gelding who was terribly neglected and needed a home. That's how we get a lot of our rental horses, sadly enough. People either come on hard times and can't pay for the substantial cost of keeping a horse or they are abusive."

"So the horse I rode yesterday had been rescued?"

"Yep. He was put in my section of the barn, so I got to befriend him and I was in charge of his care. That was five years ago now." She poked the tines of her fork into the casserole. "General was grateful for the care and kindness he received. It took him a good while to trust again, but when he did it was with his entire heart. That happens most of the time, but not with Mel. No, Mel has a mind of his own."

"In a good way, or a bad way?" He leaned toward her as if he really wanted to know.

"It's sort of mixed." She took a bite, shocked by the amazing explosion of taste on her tongue. "This is really good. As in, great. This was all in my pantry?"

"I ran to the grocery store in your truck." His

confession came quietly, almost sheepishly. "I had to test it out. Make sure the starter worked."

"Sure. So you planned this all along?"

"I had hoped to help you out, that's all, like friends do for one another all the time."

"I can't argue with that. This is amazing." She took another bite.

"Back to Mel," he prompted, although he looked pleased with her compliment. "You can't leave me in suspense."

"Mel likes to amuse himself at our expense. He's figured out that he isn't going to be hit or beat or abused no matter what he does. As if. Anyway, at first, I thought he was just testing. When I had him tied in the aisle while I cleaned his stall, he would unlatch other stalls with his teeth. I would look up and a horse would be loose—a serious thing—and he would be in their stall eating their grain."

"Sounds like a little ingenuity to me."

"I finally figured out he could untie his lead, so I had to use one with a metal hatch. Then he started nipping me when I had my back to him. When I turned around, he always stood there so innocently. So I had to tie him farther down the row, and he would practically incite a riot with the other horses while I mucked out his stall. I would have to put down my pitchfork and go see why a half dozen horses were rearing and neighing in their stalls like fire had broken out."

"He wanted your attention."

"It took me longer than you to figure that out. He was such a handful. Always knocking over any bucket he came across, making sure I got as wet as he did at bath time. I would take him out for a ride to stretch his legs and he'd take the bit between his teeth, ignore me completely and charge like a lunatic over the nearest fence. Then he would walk around, still ignoring me, arrive at the gate to be let in only to do it all over again. This was all with his good-old-boy attitude. I couldn't stay mad at him."

"He ought to jump those obstacle things. Like in competitions."

"I finally figured that out, too. He's blissfully happy carrying little students on his back over the jumps in the arena. He's a character."

"I'm not surprised you helped him to be happy again."

"I think it was his indomitable spirit." She was blushing as she speared an asparagus tip. She stared at her fork, because it was easier. If she saw the regard on Hawk's handsome face, it would affect her. She wasn't ready for that.

"Either way, it's a good story. I suppose those stables are full of them."

"Every horse, every rider." She wasn't about to bore him with a hundred horse tales. "Your turn. Tell me something about Mark Hawkins. Something that no one else knows."

"I *am* a walking mystery," he quipped, showing off that sense of humor she was fond of. The candlelight softened the hard planes of his rugged face, making him twice as striking. It was easy to imagine him in a tux and equally simple to see him suited and booted for a mission. He took a swig from his juice glass. "I want to trek through Nepal. I want to learn to play the guitar. I want to marry the love of my life and grow old with her."

"You're a romantic." The words caught in her throat. His confession moved through her, and a strong and new image tried to wedge its way into her brain, but she could not let it. She absolutely could not allow it. She reached for her juice glass to wash away all traces of emotion. "I can see you sitting on the porch with a pretty woman, both of you gray and wearing spectacles."

"I'm glad you can see it. That makes one of us. Hoping is different than believing."

Her grip slipped on her glass. The contents splashed dangerously, but she was able to set it on the table without incident. Whew. For a moment there, she thought he was talking about the two of them. But no, that was her mind at work, not his. "I'm sure it will happen for you. One day you will meet the right woman and you will know she's meant to be on that porch with you."

"I pray that you are right." He looked forlorn for a moment, as if he were afraid he would never find that right woman. As if he would never be loved. "If I can let any woman close, that is."

Sympathy rushed through her. She knew exactly how it felt to look at the future and see nothing of what once had been her deepest desire. No loving marriage, no children, no happily ever after. Life would be good and wonderful, of course, but it wouldn't be as rich without a lifetime of love and family. She didn't want that for him. "I'll keep you on my prayer list. I'm sure God has the right woman for you all picked out. It's just a matter of when."

"I'm sure that's true." He pasted on a smile, but it was only a superficial one. She was surprised love meant so much to him.

Hard not to like him more for that. She swirled

her fork and spooled pasta in slow twirls. "I tell you what. Until you find that special someone, I will be your date every New Year's Eve to come, unless you're away on a deployment, of course."

"I would like that." His grin widened, but his eyes continued to look sad, as if doubt were weighing him down. Maybe a little loneliness, too.

She knew what that was like. Her feelings took a dangerous dip. *I do not care about Hawk,* she told herself, but it was no longer the truth. She did care.

Far too much.

"I am looking forward to going back home." Hawk gave the nonstick pan a good swipe with the dish towel and pronounced it dry. He hiked over to the cabinet next to the stove and piled it into place on the shelf. "I'm especially psyched to see Pierce get married."

"You get a kick out of that, don't you?"

"I do. It's the real thing. This will work out for them. Pierce will be happy." He rejoined her at the sink and waited for the strainer she was in the middle of rinsing.

"How do you know?" She was curious. She'd

only met Tim's brother twice, but he seemed like a nice guy.

"Pierce lives for his fiancée." He took the pot lid and gave it a good rubbing. "You would like her. Her name is Lexie and she's into horses, too. She grew up with them, or something. I'll have to pay more attention next time I hear her talking about it."

He liked that his comment was met with an amused shake of her head. September smiling was what he lived for.

"I'll have to introduce you." He squinted at the lid—dry—and stowed it in the cabinet. "She's transferring from a university in Montana to go to school in Tacoma, after they get back from their Hawaiian honeymoon."

"I would love to meet her." She bent over the sink to give it a good cleaning with the dishcloth. "We could go riding together."

"See? You two will be fast friends." He hung the towel to dry on the oven handle, watching September at the sink. He grabbed the dry-erase pen hanging from the board hung by magnets on the fridge and scribbled down the right digits.

Tonight had been nice. It was as simple as pie to see how life with her would be: easygoing evenings sharing the cooking, a meal and the cleanup. They had an amicable accord, as if their personalities fit together without effort or pretense. He couldn't ever remember being this happy and centered. He had never felt so sure.

She is what I want, Lord. If it's possible. If it's Your will. The power of the prayer left him reeling. Emotion hit him harder every time he looked at her. Every time he heard her voice.

"When do you leave?"

"Tuesday." In two days. It didn't seem possible that he could tear himself away. He hated to think of it. "Hey, you wouldn't want to help me find them a wedding gift?"

"I suppose." She looked up from scrubbing. "I promised Colleen I would help out in the office, but I could meet you in the afternoon."

"Great. I could come pick you up and drag you around town."

"As long as you don't mind me doing a little shopping, too." She turned on the faucet to rinse the edges of the sink. "I've left way too much to the last minute."

"So have I."

They walked together into the living room where the Christmas tree blazed. She had added more decorations, making the scraggly tree look noble and majestic. Garlands reflected the colorful tones of the twinkle lights. A tree skirt draped over the planter added the perfect background for the small stack of wrapped gifts on the floor beneath. He had already hid his gift—a necklace of diamonds and gold in the shape of a horse—in that pile for her to discover come Christmas Day.

"I'll walk you out." She had snagged her coat from the back of the chair, and he helped her into it. Tenderness deepened again as he did this small thing for her, holding the garment, slipping it over her shoulders, gently gathering her hair to free it from the coat's collar. He wanted to always be there for her, doing what he could to make her life better.

He grabbed his coat from the entry closet where he'd hung it earlier after coming home from the grocery store, and shrugged into it. They walked out into the chilly shadows together. Walking along beneath the glow of the porch lights, he decided nothing could be nicer than to be at her side. She wasn't ready to love again, and he had a deployment scheduled in less than a month. How would this work out? He only knew one thing—he was committed to her, heart and soul, and always would be.

"I better hand over these." She scooped his keys out of her pocket. "Tell your mom when you see her that she did a good job raising you. I'm impressed."

"You really liked the tuna casserole." He chuckled, a comforting sound on a cold night. "Maybe I'll show you how to make it one day and let you discover the secret ingredients."

"What's so top secret?"

"I'm not telling you yet. You'll have to stick around to find out." He rested against the side of the truck, as if in no hurry to leave. "Look at the street. I should have asked if you wanted me to put up house lights for you."

"I don't have any. I didn't buy any last year, and this is only my second Christmas in my town house." She joined him, leaning against the pickup to gaze down the long stretch of the cul-de-sac.

Bright, colorful bulbs rimmed the rooflines of houses, dangled like icicles from porch eaves and draped over bushes and shrubs. Shining reindeer grazed and holy stars hung in front windows. A tasteful, poignant manger scene gleamed from the front lawn across the street. How had she not noticed the beauty? On some of the shortest and darkest days of winter, there was one day of perfect light.

"When I'm gone, you'll write me, won't you?" He shifted a little closer until their elbows bumped. "I noticed a computer in your family room. Hard not to notice it on the desk."

"You mean on your deployment."

"If that's not too much to ask." He cleared his throat, as if he were a little unsure. "I don't want to make you uncomfortable. I don't want to bring up anything painful for you."

"You mean all the corresponding Tim and I did when he was overseas?"

"Yep." He appeared vulnerable, something she would have thought impossible given his tough-guy character.

"No worries. I would miss you if I couldn't keep in touch. I've grown strangely fond of you."

"Strangely?" That made him laugh.

"Maybe the better word is unexpected." A little warning buzz sounded within her, but did she listen?

No. She charged right on, saying what rose on the tide of her emotions instead of sensibly censoring it. "You've changed my world, Hawk."

"The best friendships do that." His arm stayed

pressed against hers, an innocent touch and a powerful connection. One that made her feel as if her heart were threatening to open wide.

She could not let that happen. Staring off down the street, she searched for something to say that would draw back the moment, but not end it entirely. Except the silence between them felt companionable and comfortable. Maybe it would be best not to say anything more. Hawk understood they could only be friends, so why weren't her feelings agreeing?

A minivan ambled down the road and pulled into a driveway two houses down. Doors opened and a family tumbled out, the excited voices of the children ringing like carillon bells. The mom went ahead to open the front door while the dad untied the tree tied to the top of the van.

"At least you aren't the last person on your block to get a tree," he quipped, leaning a little closer. "When I get back from Wyoming, how about I help you plant it?"

"I'm pretty good with a shovel, but not so much with this cast, so I accept your offer." She couldn't help leaning into him in return.

Careful, September, she told herself, *or you will start to depend on him. And then the next thing you know, you will start needing him with every fiber of your being.*

"Look at the stars. It's a perfect night to see them, clear from horizon to horizon." Hawk gazed upward like a man comfortable with watching the heavens. She remembered that knowing how to use the stars as reference points was part of his job requirements. He turned to her, not the heavens. "It sure is beautiful to-night."

He could not be talking about her, although it felt as if he were. His caring opened her up, and she was as vulnerable as an exposed nerve. Open and tingling, overwhelmed by the emotions she could not hold back.

It is the stars, she told herself, and not this moment. Not Hawk. Not new wishes rising from the winter of the old. She simply hadn't stood out beneath the skies on a December night like this, feeling all the shades of starlight. The black sky had never looked so rich, like the perfect hue of ebony. The platinum sprinkle of stars scattered across the zenith. If she watched long enough, absorbing the brightness, she could see hints of color—of yellow, red, blue.

The kiss of the moonlight spilled from a nearly full moon, casting a shimmering path through the nearby forest and onto the black-topped street. She felt every beauty of the mountains ragged against the sky. The beauty of the night scraped against her raw senses, blissfully welcome. She remembered the girl she used to be, who believed in dreams and happily ever afters.

That girl might be worse for the wear, but she was still here, still alive, that the essential, truest part of her had not perished. She had survived the loss of a true, deep love. And while loving wasn't something she would ever risk again, she was thankful to be here beneath the magnificent sky and to have an understanding friend like Hawk. His endless kindness, his sense of humor and every good thing he had done for her made it impossible not to care about him in return. But what could come of that?

Nothing more than this moment beneath the stars. Hawk was a Ranger, as Tim had been. She could not believe her heart would ever be truly whole again. And even if by the grace of God that miracle did happen, then she would never fall for a soldier. No, not ever again.

She eased away from him, breaking their connection, shattering the moment. The stars went on burning bright anyway, and so did Hawk's friendship for her.

"I'd best get on my way and leave you to your evening." He opened his door, but his voice was no longer casual, his tone no longer easygoing. "I'll see you tomorrow."

"Tomorrow," she mumbled, stumbling up the walk. She did not wait to wave him away from her porch step. Instead, she hurried inside to close the door on what she had seen in his star-blue eyes—honest and unmistakable love for her.

Chapter Eleven

"We were lucky she's a fast healer," Patty Toppins said as she accepted a cup of tea and sat down on one of the chairs facing Colleen's desk. "She's already complaining about being stuck in the house, so I thought a little outing might perk her up."

"Good idea. I've been keeping her in my prayers, Patty." September swiveled the office chair around to face the happy mom. "You have to be incredibly relieved. I can't imagine how terrified you must have been."

"I'm better now that she's up and around. For a while there, I feared the worst. It doesn't help with the well-meaning doctors letting you know everything that can go wrong. I was a nervous wreck, but God has been watching over my girl."

"Proof prayer makes a difference." Colleen slipped into her desk chair. "The rest of the mountain is still closed. The inspection company believes there are no more covered-over mine shafts, but I'm having a second company come in just to be sure. It's not worth risking anyone's life."

"I don't know if I've thanked you for all you two have done. Colleen, covering the hospital bills like that, and you, September. I hate to think what would have happened if Crystal had been down there alone. I'll never be able to thank you for taking such good care of her in a bad situation, although I'm sorry you got injured, too."

"I only wish I could have done more." She took a sip of hot tea, wondering how events worked out the way they had. Maybe Hawk's arrival into her life hadn't been a coincidence. God was present in her life, and He had brought them together. Why? She might argue that Hawk needed her friendship as much as she needed his, but after what she'd glimpsed last night, she was pretty sure he felt more than friendship for her.

After more well-wishes, Patty left to check on her daughter, who was spending time saying hello to her beloved mare. Colleen made a call, talking seriously to the feed suppliers about price changes on their upcoming order. September signed out of the computer, one eye on the clock. Three minutes to three. Panic zinged through her veins at the thought of seeing him again.

Should she call Hawk and cancel? Pretend she hadn't noticed what looked like love in his eyes? Hope there was some other explanation for it? These questions had kept her up much of the night and plagued her all the day through. She felt torn, not knowing what to do.

She felt his presence before she saw him loping up the front steps. He gave an impressive appearance in a heather-gray army sweatshirt, jeans and combat boots and with the wind ruffling his short, dark hair. His incredible baby blues blazed a welcome as he pulled open the door. Casual, easygoing, friendly as always Hawk. Definitely not the same look as last night.

Whew. Talk about relief. She would have stood up, but her knees wouldn't work. Tension rolled through her, a sign she had been more worried than she'd realized. It must have been a trick of the moonlight, she decided. Everything looked more romantic and fanciful beneath starry skies.

"Hey, there." He ambled over to her desk. "Sergeant Hawkins reporting for duty."

"Duty?" She turned off the monitor and grabbed her purse. Funny how her knees were still quaky. "I thought we were going to the mall."

"Think of the traffic."

"True." She shuddered remembering the long lines to get in and out. She pushed out of the chair. Her knees felt tricky, but they held her weight. Odd. "This time of year, the place is packed."

"I'm a Ranger, remember?"

"As if I could forget."

"I go where all men fear to tread." He held the door for her.

Macho. She shook her head, waved goodbye to Colleen, who was still busy on the phone, and walked past him through the door. She definitely had been starstruck last night to think Mark Hawkins would fall in love with her, or with anyone. Look at him, tough as iron, undaunted and mission-focused. Hadn't he admitted last night that he had trouble letting others close?

Maybe the problem was with her, she thought. It troubled her through the drive to the freeway and the perilous ride on I-5. Hawk drove like a NASCAR racer, fast, sure and steady, competently zipping between cars, changing lanes. When the traffic slowed to a crawl near the mall, he made one final switch and she could catch her breath.

"You don't like my driving?" Amusement tugged at the corners of his mouth. "I wasn't going more than a few miles an hour over the speed limit. Gotta keep up with traffic."

"Let's just say I would rather be on a horse. I would love to drive to the store in a horse-drawn wagon."

"It would take a whole lot longer."

"Sure, but your truck is just a machine."

"Hey, it's a very nice machine." His dimples deepened, far too attractive for the man's good.

He could stop the earth with those dimples. She shook her head, hoping to dislodge the effects of his smile. What had they been talking about? Her brain seemed to have turned to fog for some inexplicable reason. Oh yes—horses versus vehicles. "I didn't say your truck wasn't nice, just that it was a machine."

Even as the sound of the words hit her ears,

she blushed. Great. Now she wasn't making any sense. She sounded like an idiot. What was wrong with her today?

Lack of sleep, she decided stubbornly. "Your truck doesn't miss you when you're gone. It doesn't snuggle with you and make you laugh. It's not your best friend. It can't love you."

"No, but I do love it." Trouble, that's what he was, and he knew it. "My truck doesn't kick me, doesn't decide to roll over in a mud puddle with me and it always does what I tell it to."

"You're using my funny stories against me." She laughed. How could she not? The man was definitely trouble of the best kind. "So you are saying convenience and control are more important than relationships."

"Do you think I'm going to say yes to that?" He kept one eye on the creeping traffic. "That is an ambush waiting to happen. I'm not about to step into that argument."

"Then that is what you think?" She could tease, too.

"If we are talking about cars, yes. I liked riding with you the other day, I won't say that wasn't one of the best days in recent times, but it would take hours to get to the mall if we decided to ride the horses."

"And you are an impatient man?"

"I can be as patient as Job if I need to be." She had no idea that was what he was determined to be. He would wait for her if it took all the days of his life. "But I'm not a fan of shopping."

"I could have guessed that. Hence, the mission talk. We get in, get out, objective accomplished."

"And no man left behind." He winked to make her laugh again, and to hide the deeper meaning, the one he could not let her guess. He would wait forever for her, he would never leave her behind. Doing his best to ignore the ever-expanding depth of his tenderness for her, he turned up an aisle of parking. "Keep a sharp eye out. Phase one in progress."

"Phase one?"

"Secure parking, then proceed to the mall."

"Phase one might take longer than the actual shopping mission." She had no idea how adorable she looked, leaning back in the seat, her hair tumbling everywhere, wearing boot-cut jeans and a Save the Whales T-shirt. "There isn't a spot anywhere."

"And a lot of competition looking." He wheeled around the end of an aisle and drove straight down the far lot. "We have an advantage."

"Oh, sure we do." She laughed at that, a musical trill that he wanted to hear forever. She twisted to get a look up the jammed aisles. "I suppose you are the advantage?"

"I was talking about being in a truck, which puts us up high so we have a better view, but sure. If you want to think of me as an advantage, I won't argue."

"You, an advantage? If I had a snowball, I would throw it at you."

"I don't think that would teach me a lesson. It would only encourage me."

"You're an incorrigible kind of guy?"

"I try to be." He caught a set of taillights flashing to life way down the row and he wheeled into the aisle. "Looks like we've got a live one."

"Could you have found a spot farther away from the mall?" Adorable how she was teasing him. You could even call it bantering. And bantering implied a certain emotional intimacy, didn't it?

A good sign, he decided as he idled in the row. The sedan inched out of the spot, the driver peering out carefully and her view probably impeded by the enormous pile of shopping bags in the backseat, and motored off. Other cars lined up, some of them oncoming, trying to beat him to the punch. He charged into the spot, beating the competition. Victory.

September shook her head as if she couldn't believe him. "I am putting that on my faults list."

"Why? What did I do?" He cut the engine and helped her with her seat belt. "I got us a spot, that's what."

"You are a barracuda, dude. I'm keeping my eye on you."

"I was here first." He could banter, too. "I didn't cut anyone off. I didn't try to steal the spot like that sports car guy. And yet you are objecting to my methods?"

"Not objecting. Just keeping watch. I think there's more than meets the eye when it comes to you."

"You have no idea." More than meets the eye? That was the truth.

He hopped down, circled around the truck, pleased to find her waiting for him. She was an independent lady, but she was letting him be her gentleman. In time, she would want more from him. He felt it all the way to his soul. He loved her. More than there were stars in the universe. Truer than there were words to say.

He hated the moment her boots touched the ground, because she let go of him.

It wouldn't always be like this. He stayed at her side as they made the trek through the parking lot, laughing all the way.

Spending time with Hawk melted her resistance. What she thought she might have seen on his face last night was forgotten. Being with Hawk in the mall was not what she expected. He was like a big kid pointing out the mall decorations lining the walkways and stopping to look in all the store displays. They'd admired endless numbers of Christmas trees, mangers, *Nutcracker* scenes, piles of beautifully wrapped gifts and hand-painted windows.

"This ought to add to our Christmas cheer." Hawk sauntered over from a coffee kiosk with two reindeer-decorated paper cups in hand. "I got an eggnog latte and a peppermint mocha. Your choice."

"There's no contest. Peppermint mocha."

"Then this is yours."

He handed her the cup with a manly flourish, and if her knees went weak again, she refused to notice. She neatly avoided contact with his fingers—just in case the strange knee reaction happened again—and took a sip of the steaming drink.

"Whipped cream. You know how to celebrate, Hawk."

"That's something I'm proud of." He joined her at the store window.

"I think that goes on the list, too."

"Not the list!" He pretended to smack the heel of his hand against his forehead. "If you keep this up, you're going to know my every shortcoming."

"True, but if you're lucky I won't hold them against you."

"Good, because I would like to stick around for a while instead of getting kicked to the curb."

No woman in her right mind would give Hawk the boot. No, certainly not judging by many appreciative looks she'd noticed other women giving him as they cruised the mall's corridors. In fact, there was another one from a woman leaving the bookstore. September sympathized. It was very hard not to notice a man who exuded honor instead of conceit, kindness instead of brashness. He studied the colorful children's books paraded up and down a stairway display. Covers of many beloved classics brought back memories.

"My dad used to read to us." He must have been feeling the same way. "He was a logger, but I think if he could have afforded college he would have been a great literature professor. Every weekend afternoon he could manage, he would be in his chair with a classic open in hand. As far back as I can remember, he would read me to sleep. He would start the Christmas stories on the first of December, my birthday. It was our tradition. Our favorite was *How the Grinch Stole Christmas*."

"One of my faves, too." It had to be the memories spearing sharp and sweetly. Overwhelmed by the intensity, she wanted to step away, put distance between them and tuck old memories back in the safe compartment she had stored them in. Surely Hawk wasn't having this effect on her emotions. "Chessie would always do the out-loud reading. She insisted. To this day, *The Night Before Christmas* does not sound right to me unless my sister is reading it."

"After my dad died, Christmas sort of fizzled in my house. Mom stopped baking and cooking. There was no Christmas candy. Liz and I had to make our own holiday. Of course, living next door to the Grangers helped."

"Tim's family." It didn't hurt to talk about them now. She meandered over to the wide breezeway where rows of books beckoned. "Tell me about your Christmases with them."

"Two Christmas trees in the house. Garland everywhere. The Grangers hang twinkle lights like you do, except on every available surface. The house smells like fresh-cut pine, baking bread and molasses cookies. Christmas music is constantly playing. Then there is the old upright piano. Everyone gathers around it on Christmas Eve and we sing until it's time to head off to the candlelight service."

"You've become part of the family."

"I needed one and they were there."

She thought of Hawk as a little boy, devastated by loss and a broken home. Her eyes burned for him. Caring spiraled within her, growing with every turn, affection she could not control. "I'm glad you have them."

"Me, too. I'm lucky they put up with me. They could take objection and put me out on the street."

"Very tempting, I'm sure."

"Hey!"

She loved how he could make her smile, how he could touch her deeply. She felt as hopeful as the stars twinkling from the overhead skylights. A mom ambled by with two small children in tow. Shopping bags crinkled, the baby clapped her hands and shouted, and the brown-haired boys toddled by, talking excitedly about Santa Claus. Want ribboned through her. She tore her gaze away and studied a book display without seeing it.

"I think I'm going to look for a home design book Chessie wants. I haven't gotten all of her gifts yet." She didn't know why she felt maudlin. Being alone was what she wanted. It was safer. She never wanted to go through the wreckage of loss again. Safer was better, even if it meant no children to fuss over and adore. Even if it meant no wonderful husband with Hawk's sense of humor and stalwart gentleness.

"Great. I'm going to need something to read for my flight." He browsed the bestsellers and chose a paperback to browse through.

She sidled over to the hardcover bestseller rack and spotted the book her sister had been salivating for. She grabbed a copy, but when she looked at the cover it was the wrong book. How had she done that?

Easy. Her gaze had glued to Hawk and refused to move. She replaced the volume, chose the right one this time and moved into the aisle toward him.

"Victory." He held up a book in triumph. "Now I won't be bored on the flight. Hey, that looks like something my mom would like. Where did you get it?"

She pointed, not quite able to make her brain find the words. Maybe it was a delayed problem from her mild concussion. It was the only reason she could think of for her sudden aphasia. She had lost motor skills, too, since juggling the coffee, her purse and the book took all her concentration. She found her credit card and handed it to the kid behind the counter. An aisle away, Hawk grabbed a book, studied it with an unassuming nod and paced her way.

Something broke apart inside her, a barrier she had constructed a long time ago. The last fortification fell. The speakers overhead sang "We Wish You a Merry Christmas," and as the clerk shoved a credit card slip at her to sign, she felt her world shift. A quiet, sacred emotion ebbed to life within her—an intense, singular brand of affection she refused to name.

Shock rocked through her. When she signed

her name, the letters were squiggly and didn't look like her writing. Hawk approached the counter and stood next to her, handing over his merchandise to a second clerk, who greeted him and began tallying his purchases.

I do not love him, she argued with herself as she shoved the pen and receipt across the counter. It was impossible for her to love him. She simply would not allow it.

"Have a nice day." Her clerk smiled at her, but his glance fell behind her shoulder, where another customer was waiting. She fumbled with the bag, the cup and her purse again, managing somehow to move out of the way.

"Great. One down, two more to go." He joined her outside the entrance. "I still haven't found the right thing for Pierce and Lexie. But we'll trek on. Our spirits are high."

What would life with Hawk be like? she wondered as they strolled to the next store. Unexpected. Joyful. Intrepid. She could not let herself picture her future with him. They were friends, nothing more. She would tell herself that until it was totally, entirely true.

"You're looking a little pale. Are you feeling okay?"

"F-fine." She *was*. There was no other alternative. "Where to next?"

"Look. A Christmas tree." Hawk turned to the banister, gazing at the floor below where Santa sat in a red velvet chair and a long line of kids and parents waited to see him. In the middle of the plaza winked an enormous tree, dazzling with cheer and cuteness. But that wasn't the tree Hawk pointed toward.

Across the way, in a nearly bare storefront, was a wishing tree, decorated with slips of paper hung by colorful ribbons. Most shoppers hurried by, without giving it a second glance. "Let's go shopping for some kids. Want to?"

The words disappeared again. She nodded, struggling not to feel. She had to resist whatever this was threatening to take her over.

"Great. Mom always included gifts for the church's charity tree in our Christmas traditions. After she lost interest in celebrating, my sis and I kept it up." He laid a hand on her shoulder, gently guiding her through an oncoming throng of teenagers. "It's something I do whenever I'm Stateside in December."

"You know me. I think it's a great idea. Chessie and I do the same thing for our church tree." Her head rang but she was able to speak and walk at the same time. A major accomplishment considering the intensity of these new feelings. She was only slightly preoccupied as they searched through the names hanging on the charity tree. She watched him through the thick, fragrant boughs, concentrating as he read several requests, his amused reactions and the excitement on his rugged face.

"Here's one. I'm taking it." He unhooked a paper slip. "This kid would like a big yellow dump truck. As I'm especially fond of dump trucks, I know just what he wants."

"I can see you as a little boy playing on a mound of dirt with your construction trucks." Not hard at all to picture how cute he would have been, his dark hair longer and wind tousled, that cowlick at the crown of his head more pronounced. And those big blue eyes probably made his mom melt every time he trained them on her to ask for something. How could anyone say no to a face like that?

"What do you have there?" He sidled around the tree, sneaking dangerously close so that he could read the paper she held. "Oh, baby dolls. I have no experience there."

"You had a sister. Didn't she have dolls?"

"Well, let me rephrase that. I wasn't exactly

honest. My sole experience with dolls is very limited. Mostly hostage taking, kidnapping, ransom demanding-type missions." He looked sheepish. "And before you say it, yes, I got into trouble big-time. Mom said a corner in the house is worn out because I spent so much time in it."

"You? Getting in trouble? I can't picture it." They laughed together.

"It's true. One corner of the living room is really dingy from me leaning against it all those years. I'm guessing you never got into trouble."

"I never got very far being troublesome." This man could make her laugh as nobody could. "Chessie was on the case. She was a very watchful big sister. The minute I stepped a toe out of line she was off to tell Mom about it."

"Got to keep those younger siblings in line." They laughed harder.

She pocketed the child's name and searched for another. She didn't know how it had happened, or the exact moment her soul had healed, but she was living again and laughing. If she was happy, that meant she could be hurt, too. She plucked another name off the tree blindly, her hand trembling. She didn't want any more pain in life. She did not want to risk falling in love before she realized it.

Next to her Hawk chuckled at something he read. "This kid wants a big package of candy all to himself so his big brother can't steal it from him. I'm surprised they wrote that on the request card. I'm going to find the best selection of chocolate and box it up for this fella. As penance for all the times I stole things from my little sister."

She shook her head, liking him more by the minute. He would be a tough man not to fall for, and she refused to do it. Whatever happened, she would not surrender her heart to him.

Chapter Twelve

"I'm going to put this up right now." Hawk tugged the store bag from his truck's backseat. September's street was alive tonight, with a caroling group serenading at the far end of the cul-de-sac. "Every other house has got at least one outside decoration up."

"It's late, Hawk. I'll go plug in my tree lights and it will be festive enough. You don't have to go to the trouble." Cute. She really thought he would opt out?

"It'll be fun." He intended to stay until the job was done. There was more decorating to do. He was no quitter. "Hey, there. What do you think you're doing?"

"Uh, getting my shopping bags."

"No, you aren't." He couldn't believe her. He grabbed her bags before she could. "Please go turn on the porch light so I don't trip over my own feet."

"That's something an Army Ranger does a lot? Trip in the dark?"

"If I did, I wouldn't be very good at my job."

"So why did you say that?" She searched through her keys, but he caught her watching him.

Nice. Maybe things were progressing better than he thought. "I just wanted to make you laugh, sunshine."

"And why is that?"

"Because when you're happy, I'm happy." He followed her up the steps and into the house. "Where do you want these?"

"Just put them anywhere." She dropped her purse on the coffee table and hit the switch. Merry lights blazed on the little tree, chasing away the dark. She whirled to face him, more beautiful to him by the moment.

Yep, he was definitely in big trouble here. With every passing second, he loved her more. He didn't know love could do that, increase exponentially until it felt too big to hold and too impossible to believe. But standing here with her *was* real.

"Look." He pointed to the ceiling. "Mistle-toe."

"How convenient. You decided to stand there on purpose."

"True, but that doesn't change the fact. We have to kiss." He hauled her into his arms while the tree lights blinked as if in agreement. "Tradition."

"And you think I'm a traditional girl?"

"I know you are." The evening had been the best of his life. Being in her company, talking and laughing, had been priceless. Infinitely tender, he lowered his lips to hers. Just one brush of a kiss, that was all he meant, because he didn't want to pressure her to feel something too soon. That might frighten her. He would die before he hurt her or scared her in any way.

Yep, he meant the kiss to be one light tender caress. Chalk it up to good intentions. But her fingers curled around his as if she were holding on, as if she were swept away, too, by the incredible evening and the closeness they'd shared.

When he broke the kiss, he thought he saw an answering affection on her dear face, but then she spun away and her hair hid her expression like a curtain, shielding him.

I love her so much, Lord. His heart opened wide with prayer and thanksgiving. *Thank You for this time with her.* Loving her was the sweetest thing he'd ever known.

All his life he had worked at keeping a safe distance between him and everyone else. His best buds and lifelong friends, Pierce and Tim, had gotten the closest. But that was friendship. This—his chest swelled, his soul expanded— this was something else entirely. Wonderful. Scary. Amazing. She *had* to love him back—in time. She was his future, his beloved, his everything. He knew it beyond all doubt.

"I'm going to go put up your new yard decorations." His cheerful step knelled in the shadows. "Now you won't be the Scrooge of the neighborhood."

"I didn't know I was." Chuckling, she followed him to the door, but he was already hiking down the walkway, at one with the dark. She flipped on the porch light, realizing she'd forgotten that earlier. Probably because Mark Hawkins scrambled her brains. He short-circuited her system. His kiss was such perfection, it erased the memory of all other kisses that had come before and made her want to dream about a future with him—not that she was going to.

No, there would be no dreaming allowed.

"Where do you want 'em?" He kept just out of reach of the light like an intruder clinging to the shadows, like a thief come to steal her heart.

He was talking about decorations, and she was trying to hold on to her careful emotional balance. The foundation on which she had built the last two years of her life. She rubbed her forehead, fighting to think.

"I'll try it along the walkway first, yeah?" Unaware of her struggle, he ripped open the box, the cracking sound of hard plastic ricocheted in the quiet. He extracted a stack of stars and their long white connecting cord. "If I march them across the lawn, they might compete with the tree. I have to say, that tree does look good from here. You know how to pick 'em."

Could she banter back with him? No, because she couldn't think of a single thing to say. Her brain had ground to a halt out of sheer panic. Neither could she move out of the doorway. She stood half in, half out. The cool night air danced over her and she shivered.

"That doesn't look half bad." The shadow in her yard stopped to study his work. One white star rose up out of her flower bed. Hawk gave it an adjustment, as if it wasn't standing straight enough for him.

You would think being unable to see him in the dark would make it easier. But no, her mind—the one that couldn't think of a single word in the English language—remembered every line and hollow of his face, every curve and edge. She didn't need light to know that with the angle of his jaw, he was frowning. And because he was thinking something through, a handsome crinkle would dig into his forehead.

That man could make her forget. He could make her want to believe. For a few hours tonight, he had. She had been like Cinderella at the ball, feeling beautiful as if she were in a gown and slippers, princess quality with a real live prince on her arm. Sure, they were only shopping, not dancing at a fancy ball, but the feeling was the same. The kiss had sealed it.

She didn't want to stop believing—not yet. She wanted this evening with him to go on forever. Laughing in his truck, shopping on his arm, choosing dolls and trucks in the toy store with Hawk at her side had made her happy and alive and full of hopeful joy. Hawk's kiss made her whole, even in the places she thought would always be scarred. New and powerful feelings beat against her defenses, wanting to be set free. Hawk had done this. He had walked into her life and made her love him.

No, she thought. *I do not love him. I will not love him. I am in control of my heart.*

"Hey, beautiful. What do you think?" He stood on the lawn, graced by the jewel tones of the Christmas tree winking through the window. He looked like a gift. He was everything she thought she would never find. Everything she was terrified of losing again.

"Just need to plug these in." Like the athlete he was, he stalked through the flower beds, hurdled the porch rail and snaked the cord through the railing posts. Red, gold, blue and green light dappled him as he knelt in front of the big picture window. The stars on the lawn burst into majestic white, glowing with steady promise. He bounded to his feet. "Mission accomplished."

"You were right. Those look great in the yard." The decorations shone like hope in the dark, light chasing away the clutches of an endless night.

"Sure you don't want any house lights?" He strolled toward her, fully illuminated, everything revealed—the crease in his forehead, the affection in his eyes and the memory of their kiss on his lips. "I could come back with a ladder."

Why couldn't she stop thinking about that kiss? Because it hadn't been a friendly kiss. It had nothing to do with mistletoe and tradition and everything to do with what was budding between them. A romance.

She wanted to deny it. Friendship was not necessarily romance. Going Christmas shopping wasn't specifically dating. But that kiss, that *had* been romantic. Sweetly, softly romantic.

"I could come back with dinner. Maybe I could grab some takeout." Hawk leaned against the railing, appearing casual. But he wasn't. He was asking her out on a date. On *another* date.

Just as today had been. Fear raked through her. She stumbled and grabbed the door frame for support. Her mind raced over all the times she and Hawk had been together—he'd brought flowers to the hospital, pizza to her house and flowers to dinner. He'd taken her out to eat, gone riding with her, told her about what he wanted from life—marriage and a family one day. That was not only dating behavior, but courting talk.

"September, are you all right?" Concerned,

he came to her, his hands curling around the curve of her shoulder, his tall shadow falling across her, obliterating the light.

All right? She thought he needed her friendship. She certainly needed his. But that had been a fool's path. From the moment he took her hand in the mine shaft, she had never been the same.

"Hawk, you are asking to come over with dinner out of friendship, right?" Her hands came up to land on his chest of their own volition. She ignored the secure feeling of being in his arms and the reliable thump of his heartbeat beneath her palms. "It's not a date?"

"Well, that depends." His baritone dipped deep and low, infinitely tender. So tender it made every part of her soul want to dream of him. His grip on her tightened slightly, as if he wanted to draw her closer, but held back. "It can be a date if you want it to be."

"What does that mean?" Confusion ripped through her. "Either it's a date or it isn't. Either we have a friendship or we don't."

"It doesn't have to be that black and white. Couldn't we just hang out and see where this goes? I don't think we need to worry about labeling or examining it."

"Then basically you are saying yes. It is a

date. You just don't want to call it that." She
started to shake, feeling vulnerable as if a ledge
at her feet had given way and she was falling.
The painful crash was only a matter of time. A
painful, shattering strike of bone to earth and
rock that would destroy her all over again. Love
hurt. It was as simple as that. Life was uncertain at best, and she did not have the strength
to hurt like that again.

"It's a friendly date." Ever gentle, Hawk didn't
push. Calm, he didn't move toward her to pull
her closer into his arms. Nor did he let go of her.
"I want to see you again, September. I want to
hang with you."

"You're trying to make this casual, but it's
not." She could see it now. A plea resonated in
the cool air around them, a silent emotion she
could feel from his spirit to hers. She could not
deny the connection between them. A mysteri-
ous bond she had never had with Tim or anyone. A tie she had to break. "I agreed to being
friends. You know that."

"Have I ever asked anything of you other than
friendship?"

No, she answered truthfully. But there was
one thing that had not been friendship for her.
"That kiss. That was not friendly. It might have

started out that way, but it wasn't how I ended up feeling."

"I didn't intend for things to go from friendly to serious in five seconds flat." Sincere, ever honest, that was Hawk. "I'm sorry if it was too fast. We can hit the brakes. Keep it casual."

"Go back to being friends?"

"Whatever you want, September. As long as you please let me stay in your life." He didn't falter, he didn't back down. "That's all I'm asking for."

"You mean that's all you're asking for right now?"

"Yes." He winced, as if telling the truth cost him. "I'm here as a friend, September. Nothing more."

"But you feel more?"

"I can't say that I don't." Tension corded in his neck. That had to hurt, too. "Can you say the same?"

No, she couldn't. The truth lodged in her throat, refusing to budge. This was only going to end in sorrow. She knew that for a fact. He should know what he was asking of her. He towered before her, everything she wanted, everything she was afraid to lose.

No, she couldn't hurt like that again. She

couldn't take that risk. It hurt too much. She could not go back to worrying through every deployment and expecting the worst to happen again. And what if it did? What if she gave in, fell in love only to lose him? How could she pick up those pieces a second time? She was not that strong. She wanted to be.

She wasn't.

"I wish I could be who you need me to be." Her voice wobbled dangerously. She willed down every feeling, every affection until she was a part of the shadows. She felt the star shine fade, every bit of bright light and every twinkle until only darkness remained. She had to be honest. She had to do the right thing. "But I can't be. You know what I've lost. We can only be friends."

"Only?" No emotion passed across his face. "Maybe we can agree to keep things friendly. We don't have to put time limits or constraints on it."

"I need them, Hawk. Don't you see? I can't let myself care for you more than that." She pulled away from him as if being near to him tortured her. As if he had hurt her beyond repair.

"But friendships can deepen." At least he prayed it would. *This is in Your hands, Lord,*

*but please, if it's Your will, let this work out.
Let her love me.*

All he wanted was the chance to win her heart. Just the chance.

But even he could see it was too late.

"I didn't want you as anything more than a friend." Terribly gentle came her words, laced with genuine affection. "You knew this from the start. I'm sorry, but I am never going to love you. It's not a possibility."

"Wow." A puff of air escaped him, otherwise he couldn't move, couldn't breathe. He felt frozen from the impact of her words. That happened in a serious injury, he knew from firsthand experience. The pain was too much for the body to tolerate, the shock too great for the nervous system. First came a vast, stunning stillness, which he was experiencing. Proof that he'd come to love her more than he'd realized. Then pain crashed through him like a bomb strike—a polite bomb strike. Apology was etched into her beautiful face, along with concern for him.

But there was more. He could feel her agony. This was hurting her. *He* was hurting her. The devastation felt like a death blow. He steeled his spine and pretended he was fine. This was no big deal. She didn't need to feel sorry; she'd been honest. A man couldn't ask for more than that. He pasted what he hoped was a good-natured look on his face. "I heard you loud and clear, September. Message received."

"I'm sorry to be so blunt." More than apology crinkled adorably around her pretty mouth and luminous eyes. "I don't mean to be. This isn't easy."

"You're hurting. I'm hurting. This is not what I want. It's not why I'm here. If I'm not making you happy—"

"You should leave," she finished his thought, completed his sentence and looked as broken up as he felt.

Everything inside him screamed to go to her, to draw her into his arms, cradle her to his chest and comfort her. Make this better for her. But how could he go against her wishes? No, he had to turn away. He had to walk off, knowing his love caused her pain.

His boots rang on the porch boards—a hollow sound. The tree lights blazed through the window, as if nothing catastrophic had happened. A car rolled down the street behind them. The carolers' tune grew louder as they stopped at the house next door, singing about rockin' around the Christmas tree. And September backed through her doorway, standing there like the other times she had wished him good-night. One horrible thing was different—the way she looked at him with utter misery.

It wasn't good-night this time. It was good-bye.

"Thanks for the good day." His steps drummed on the stairs. "I will remember it for a long time."

"Me, too." She didn't move from the doorway. She couldn't. "Thanks for everything you've done for me. I want you to know that it mattered."

"I'm glad. Then it was all worth it." He raised his hand in one sweeping wave for goodbye. Maybe he couldn't say the words, either. He pivoted on his heel and strode away, straight shouldered, noble, infinitely strong.

She hated seeing him go. It was killing her. She gripped the door, unable to close it, unable to deprive herself of the last look she would have of him. Watching him walk away was the hardest thing she had done since burying Tim. She felt broken all over again. There was no way to shield herself from the truth. She was not the same woman she'd been when she'd tumbled down that forgotten mine shaft. She was someone healed, someone hopeful, someone who longed to dream again.

She longed to love him, truly and deeply for the rest of her life, but he was a Ranger, in and out of danger. She could not do it. She could not face that again. Not even for him. No one, especially not she, was strong enough for that.

She heard his truck door close and the engine roar to life. She watched him drive away, her every cell, her every neuron, her very essence shrieking at her to go after him.

She didn't. He disappeared into the night, gone forever from her life. As the carolers harmonized "We Wish You a Merry Christmas," she bowed her head, overwhelmed with misery.

Black clouds rolled in from the coast, grabbing the starlight and stealing it like a thief in the dark. Hawk grabbed the shopping bags from the backseat and shouldered the door shut. The parking lot was still and silent; a few lights blazed in the base apartments. A faint drone of voices and music rose as he hoofed it up the front steps. The complex's Christmas party. He'd totally forgotten.

Not that he was in a social mood. No, he was

pretty much toast. September didn't want him.
She'd told him so. She was never going to love
him. That would never be a possibility.

Never was a harsh word. With every step he
took down the hall, the pain set in deeper. With
every crinkle and rustle of the bags came a reminder of their evening together: September's
blazing joy in front of the Christmas books,
the prowl for a parking spot and all the fun little things they had shared, his hunt for change
through his pockets for the Salvation Army donation pot. Dinner at the food court where he
ate ten tacos—she'd counted in disbelief. How
she'd tuned his truck radio—and he let no one
mess with his radio—to some frilly station
where Christmas music played 24/7 and they
sang along with the carols to while away the
time trying to get out of the mall parking.

Yeah, good job at not remembering, Hawk.
He took the stairs at the far end of the hall, so he
could avoid the loud common room where, judging by the sound of things, the party was in full
swing. A singing competition of "The Twelve
Days of Christmas" rang along the empty cor-
ridor as he hit the stairwell. Laughter and mer-
riment followed him like a dog on a trail.

Never, she'd said. She would never love him.
She might as well have taken a knife to his soul.

He charged into his place and shut the door.
Darkness met him. The bags gave a final rustle as he dropped them to the floor. He didn't
bother with the light. Finding his way by memory, he headed straight to the fridge, cracked
open a can of soda and hiked out onto the bal-
cony. Cold met him, and he welcomed it. With
any luck, it would numb the agony threatening
to overtake him. He could freeze his emotions
enough so he would never feel the pain of September's rejection.

He eased into a frosty deck chair, planted
his elbows on his knees and stared off into the
night. Only a few stars remained, the rest of
the sky loomed inky-black, heavy with a coming storm. Faint sounds from the party down
below drifted up to him like a carol. He took
a swig of soda and tuned out the music, too.
Did it work? No, because the music looped him
back to standing on September's yard getting
the new decorations just right. Why had he let
her so far in? It was a doomed mission—he
could have seen it rationally. He was always
going to get hurt.

"Hawk, you in here?"

He squeezed his eyes shut for a moment, drawing up his reserves, burying his hurt. By the time Reno found him, he'd been able to wipe the grief from his face.

"Why aren't you at the party?" Reno leaned against the frame of the slider door. "I came to fetch you earlier, but you were out."

"Christmas shopping. I head home tomorrow morning."

"I know. I'm your ride to the airport, remember? You look like you could use some cheering up. Some of the new recruits are going to put on some kind of Christmas skit. It's supposed to be a riot. You don't want to miss that."

"Right." He took another slurp of cola. "I'll be down in a bit."

"Something wrong, buddy?"

"Nothing I can't handle." It was true. He would face the pain. He was a Ranger; he didn't go around, he went through. He didn't give up and he didn't give in. Right now, he couldn't see there was any other alternative. September didn't want him. He had moved too fast too soon.

"Okay. I'll come fetch you for the skit." Reno sounded unsure, as if he were starting to figure out something wasn't right.

"I'm good," he assured his buddy. "Go back to the party."

"I'll see you there, then. Did you hear? Word is, our deployment's been moved up."

Hawk managed to nod. As Reno headed for the exit, he took another swallow of soda. So much for being alone. He couldn't miss the obligatory production by the newbies, but he didn't feel like being around a lot of people, either. All he wanted was September.

He'd scared her with that final kiss and he lost his only chance with her. She was his light in the dark and always would be. Grief grabbed at him, shadowed and all-consuming. She had been the one he'd let too close. Funny how he hadn't even realized it. It just happened. And now look at the result. He was sitting alone in the night without her.

She watched the last stars wink out, and she felt hopeless. She'd cried until there were no more tears, and that made no sense. She didn't love Hawk. Losing him shouldn't hurt like this.

She shifted on the window seat, the house dark and quiet around her. The entire world had gone still, as if the earth had stopped spinning.

The sweet memory of their kiss remained like a treasure she could not relinquish.

She leaned her forehead against the cold glass, wishing she could turn back time and bury herself in ice. If she were numb, she wouldn't have to feel the keen-edged pain of breaking Hawk's heart. She wrapped her arms around her middle, trying to comfort herself, but the pain remained.

She relaxed into the window-seat cushions, the rustling movements echoing in her solitary family room. She had gotten carried away tonight. Caught up in a rare happiness, she had forgotten to hold back, to keep Hawk at a distance. She hadn't realized her emotions were threatening to get away from her.

Good thing she caught it when she did before she started dreaming of Hawk as her husband one day, of the happy marriage and the kids they would have. Two little boys—her rebellious, foolish mind could almost see them— and a little girl who loved horses. Dreams she could not give in to, but it was too late. Their seeds had already taken hold, and she would be haunted by their promise for the rest of her life.

Raindrops struck the window and slid down the dark glass. More followed behind them, tapping a lonely melody. A few moments later water gurgled in the gutters and the lilac bushes began to sway, their branches whispering against the siding. She couldn't help wondering if Hawk was watching the rain fall and if he were thinking of her, too. She thought so. It was as if emotion connected them across the miles, and she could sense his hurt, as bleak as her own.

Don't think of him, September. She rose from the cushions, walking through the dark room to the kitchen, where the faint blink of colored lights grew stronger with every step. The dear little tree with its nonproportional branches and lopsided trunk stood proudly at the window, limbs raised toward heaven. With the star topper blazing, the fir looked like grace itself, transformed by the light, a symbol of grace.

I cannot love him. She touched a featherlike needle and drew in the tree's comforting pine scent. Hawk was a soldier. As a Ranger, he put himself in harm's way every time he went on a mission. The thought of losing Hawk fractured her in pieces. Proof that it was too late for friendship. Her affections ran too deep. Life for a soldier was too uncertain and her heart too fragile. She had to let him go.

Help me to be strong, Lord, and to do the right thing. She gazed skyward, but heaven felt far away on this desolate night.

Chapter Thirteen

"You look terrible." Chessie marched across the cathedral's parking lot, her heels tapping a no-nonsense rhythm. They came every year for the seasonal performance. "Did you sleep at all last night? It's your arm. It's hurting you."

"Stop, my arm is fine." September wasn't about to admit why she had tossed and turned all night. "It was just one of those nights. You look gorgeous. Is that a new dress?"

"An impulse buy when I was shopping for Evelyn." Chessie gave a flourish, showing off the flowing silk garment beneath her equally tasteful wool coat. "You know how I am about sticking to budgets, but it was on sale and I fell in love with it."

"Do you know what that would be great for?

Your New Year's Eve date." They followed the sidewalk to the church's wide steps.

"That's what I thought, too." Chessie paused to take two programs from the stand in the vestibule and handed one over. "So, how did your shopping expedition with Hawk turn out?"

"How did you—?"

"Ha! Colleen told me. I stopped by to see Princess. I don't think she meant to tell. She assumed I knew all about the new man in your life."

"He's not in my life." Especially after last night. Battling regret, she forged ahead down the aisle, ignoring the beautiful glasswork and the discordant notes of the orchestra warming up. She pointed to an available pew toward the middle. At Chessie's nod, she eased into the row, praying that her sister would drop the subject and knowing she would not.

"I thought things were going well." Her sister looked chagrined as she settled onto the bench. "You were spending a lot of time together."

"*Were* being the operative word. He left for Wyoming this morning."

"Well, it's still early. You can call him before you get home. It's what, only an hour ahead in Wyoming? It won't be too late."

"You want me to call him? I thought you didn't like him." She unbuttoned her coat, paying a lot of attention to each button. The one thing she could not do was to think about Hawk's laugh, or his undying optimism, or his kiss. What she especially could not afford to do was to imagine the dreams lost, pictures of a future with him.

"I told you. I don't like what he does, but look at you. If this is how much you miss him when he leaves, it's too late for my opinion. Your heart has already decided. You are in love with him."

"I am not." That came out defensively. Out of the corner of her eye she saw people two pews away turn to look at her. She lowered her voice. "Hawk and I aren't a couple, trust me."

"But you want to be?"

"No." *But we could have been.* Regret battered her. Everything inside her shouted out for him. She stowed her purse on the floor beneath the pew, doing her best not to look at Chessie. She did not want her sister to guess what had happened. "I can't fall for another Ranger. I knew it all along. You do, too, remember? You told me from the start. But—"

She hung her head, unable to admit it was already too late. She felt her sister's concern like the draft from the wide-open doors. Rustling started as the choir filed onto the bleachers at the head of the church. Soon the program would start and that would put an end to this discussion.

But not to her misery. Why couldn't she forget what it had been like to be cared for by him? If only she could forget the time they had spent together—picking out the tree, doing dishes, sipping hot coffee. It wasn't as if he had whisked her off to Paris. He had simply taken her to the mall. So why was she hung up on him? Why couldn't she bear to let a single memory of him go?

The conductor tapped his baton against the podium, and the cathedral quieted in anticipation. She tried to silence the whisperings in her mind. She tried to quiet her unmistakable sadness. The first majestic notes of Handel's *Messiah* blasted into the sanctuary, but the music didn't touch her. "Hallelujah," the choir belted out in perfect harmony, but it might as well have been silence. The beautiful, inspiring music did not touch her. It did not uplift her. It did not make her want to believe.

I'm grieving him, she realized. She hadn't imagined that love could come again into her heart. She had mistaken friendship for something more. She had ignored her deepening feelings when she should have been honest enough to examine them. As the music crescendoed and the joy of the music reverberated in the acoustic glory of the cathedral, she was in silence. The only music she heard was longing within her soul for a lifetime with Hawk. For one brief second, she saw what could be—frequent laughter and quiet moments, a lifetime spent with his companionship and his stalwart, ever-caring love. Children and birthdays and celebrations. Grandchildren and retirement. Evenings spent on a porch. A love that strengthened day by day.

A wish was all it could be, a daydream and nothing more.

Chessie leaned close to whisper, "Are you all right?"

"I will be." She set her chin, fixed her eyes on the choir and tried to let the music carry her away. She had to be practical. She might want that future with Hawk, but she was not a woman who could afford to dream. End of story. The fall that followed love lost was not worth it.

Wait a minute. Did that mean she would rather have never met Tim? That she would have been better off never loving him? No. Her life was richer—she was richer—because the sweet, enthusiastic idealistic Tim Granger had come into her life. So that made her wonder. What would she miss with Hawk?

She hung her head, realizing that was one question she would not have answered. Remembering the look on his face, it was over. She was too late.

Sorrow hit her with a bleak punch, unfair on an evening so beautiful in a sanctuary fraught with light and glorious in song.

"You've been awfully quiet tonight." Frank Granger, Pierce's uncle, drew up a chair and hunkered down beside him at the cloth-covered table. The extended family had moved into the living room to pour over old wedding albums.

Hawk didn't have the will to join them. All through the wedding talk, rehearsal and rehearsal dinner, he couldn't help wondering about his future—the one he wanted more than air to breathe. An impossible future. He should have known that all along. He could have saved himself a passel of disappointment.

"Just got a lot on my mind." He grabbed the can of root beer he'd been working on and upended it. Drained the last of the soda in three gulps.

"When a man looks like you do, it's always woman trouble." There was no pulling the wool over Uncle Frank's eyes. He was a widower who ran a successful ranch north of Jackson Hole. It was hard not to like Frank. He was the sort of man who looked you in the eye when he talked to you, a man who always did the right thing. Hawk had known him since he was a boy and respected him more with each passing year.

"If I tell you you're right, that I've got some major woman trouble, then you will want to know about it." He set down the can and pushed back his chair.

"We don't have to talk about it." Frank reached across the table to steal a carrot stick left on the vegetable plate from dinner. "Sometimes it's best to let things simmer. If you think on it long enough, the right answer will come to you."

"I appreciate that. But I doubt there's a right answer."

"There's always a right answer, son."

"No, it's definitely over." Miserable, Hawk snatched a carrot stick, too, and crunched on it. "She dumped me."

"That hangdog look on your face can only mean one thing." Frank looked as if he had seen it all. "I was a married man for a long time. I know what a woman can do to a man's heart."

"It's my fault. Not hers." That was the worst part. He'd known how she felt and yet he went charging ahead like a good Ranger. But he forgot sometimes you got further by sitting tight. "I fell in love with Tim's ex-fiancée."

"You sure know how to find trouble, don't you?" Frank finished off his carrot stick and stole a radish off the platter. "It takes time to get over a loss like that. The more the girl loved him, the longer it's gonna take and the harder it is."

"I know. I moved too fast. I thought she felt the same way, or close enough." His guts twisted and he tossed the carrot stick onto his abandoned dinner plate.

"The thing about women is that you can never tell what they're thinkin'. They will surprise us men every time. I can see this girl means something real to you."

"As real as it gets." The conversation in the living room crescendoed into a roar. Laughter, playful shouting and Mrs. Granger's drill sergeant voice echoed through the house. Even

Roger, the old sheepdog, added a *woof! woof!* as if cheering someone on. Pierce and his brother were probably wrestling in the house—something crashed to the floor. Yep, and now they were getting into trouble.

"That's no way for you boys to behave on the night before a wedding. *Your* wedding, Pierce. I'm not sure you are mature enough to get married after this." Beneath the firm layer of stern in Mrs. Granger's tone was suppressed laughter. "Sean, I can't believe you. Get off the floor and pick that up. You're lucky nothing broke. Now straighten up, both of you."

"Yes, ma'am," two voices answered in unison, stuttering laughter.

Hawk shook his head. Time passed, one year blurring into the next, but some things stayed the same. The Granger family would always be just like this, even without Tim. It heartened him to know love went on, and that families could survive. Maybe if he gave her enough time—

"This girl you're in love with. You want to marry her?" Frank broke into his thoughts.

"More than anything on this earth."

"You're the man. It's up to you to convince her of that." He leaned back in his chair, nibbling on the radish. He nodded in the direction of the kitchen doorway. "Hello there, Giselle."

"I didn't mean to interrupt." Pierce's little sister padded into the room. The dark-haired college-age sweetheart was going to break a lot of hearts one day. "I wanted to get a start on the dishes. Mom and Lexie did all this cooking and baking. Mom's tired, and Lexie is getting married tomorrow. They should not have to do the dishes."

"I agree. Let me pitch in. Make myself useful for a change." Wry-humored, Frank pushed out of his chair. "Hawk, listen. I've thought this through. You are a Ranger. Tim was a Ranger. Is that the problem?"

"It sure is." His guts coiled tighter. "Plus, I think she's afraid to love anyone again."

"Most of us don't want to walk a path that we're afraid of alone." He grabbed a few plates to stack. "Maybe she needs you more than you think."

"Maybe." Stoneware clinked and clattered as Giselle rinsed dishes and stacked them in the dishwasher. He pushed away from the table, scooped up as many glasses as he could carry and followed Frank to the sink. Music vibrated from the front room—Mrs. Granger was playing the piano. The simple melody of "Silver Bells" was drowned out by the Granger family's singing.

He wished September were here. Regret choked him. He wished he had held back on that kiss. He wished he could change her fear. He didn't know how to fix it. Uncle Frank had to be right—he was always right. What was the solution? How was he going to try to win back a woman who'd admitted she would never love him?

He missed her so much, it was a physical pain. A blade-sharp incision digging into his guts. An emptiness in his soul he couldn't heal. She touched him deeply, where no one ever had before. She turned him inside out and upside down, and yet her softest touch made peace settle within him. She was the reason he drew breath. This was no ordinary love. Not for him.

This was a divine gift. The chance for a truly special love. How could he walk away from that?

"Hey, Frank, get in here!" Mr. Granger called out to his brother, when the song ended. "You and Carol can play duets, and we'll all sing along."

"Oh boy, I knew this was gonna happen." Pretending to grumble, Frank carried one last load to the sink. "You look like a man who needs a dose of Christmas spirit. C'mon, Giselle, Hawk. We'll do these later."

Looked as though he wasn't going to be able to avoid the family—usually the one thing he looked forward to the most when he came home. Mom was sitting on the couch, cradling a cup of tea, the fireplace crackling merrily in the hearth nearby. She smiled at him and patted the cushion at her side. As Mrs. Granger made room on the piano bench and Frank gave the ivories a tickle, he gave the sheepdog a head pat and dropped down next to his mom.

"You've been awfully quiet tonight," she observed. "You aren't coming down with something, are you?"

"Nothing a good night's sleep won't cure." That was true enough. He'd hardly slept a wink last night. He feared tonight he would be doing the same. Twisted up over September, unable to fix what was wrong, looking at his future without her.

The piano burst into life, cheerfully banging out the first notes to "Jingle Bells," and everyone in the room sang along with the melody. The room was crowded—besides Pierce's family, all of Frank's grown kids circled around the piano. The younger cousins from the other uncle had settled on the floor. The fire crackled, the Christmas tree glistened and snow gusted against the big bay window.

In the center of the room sat the happy couple. Pierce, looking pretty satisfied, had his arm around his bride. Tomorrow at two o'clock in the century-old church in town, they would join their lives as one. They were going to be happy. He was happy for them. Couldn't happen to a better couple, but all this true love and happily ever after made him think of what he had lost.

September. Somehow he would go on without her, not that it would be easy. She hadn't lost her heart, the way he had. He still loved her. It was as if his heart could not help feeling hers, and his caring unstoppable. What was the right thing to do? Did he turn away from her or help her?

He lifted his voice in song with the others, but his spirit wasn't in it.

Chapter Fourteen

Rain pinged off the windshield of September's truck as she pulled into the riding stable's graveled lot. It was still early on Christmas Eve morning and the place was quiet. She eased to a stop next to Colleen's SUV. Sitting in this truck was a constant reminder of Hawk. Every time she started the engine and it turned over without a hitch, she had him to thank.

It wasn't only the truck. Every time she walked beneath the gutter, it didn't leak. Every time she turned on her Christmas tree lights. Every time she saw those stars lighting up her front yard at night. She thought of him, the man she had sent away. He'd gone home to his family. Soon he would be deploying to a war zone. He was out of her life for good.

That was what she wanted, right? She didn't

know anymore. The thought of never seeing him again killed her. An iron band had cinched around her ribs, squeezing tighter and tighter with every memory he'd left her.

Pain she had not been able to drive from her heart. She had sent him away thinking it was the one way to protect herself from pain, but she had been wrong. She yearned to see his rugged face, to hear the deep notes of his voice, to feel safe and protected and whole again whenever he towered at her side.

Stop thinking of him, September. She launched out of the truck and closed the door with a bang that echoed like a gunshot in the nearly empty lot. A few vehicles were parked near the barn's entrance. The car and SUV she recognized as belonging to owners dropping by to ride their horses, but the white pickup sure looked like Hawk's.

Don't be silly, she told herself. All she could see was the top of the cab and the truck's bed. Plenty of people drove white trucks. It wasn't his. Hawk wouldn't come back to Fort Lewis until after Christmas and his trek in the backcountry. Gravel crunched beneath her boots, and she swiped rain from her face. Disappointment sank through her. Proof how badly she cared for him.

Be honest, September. You don't just care for him.

A movement caught her eye, a flash of red in the gray rain. A man's shadowed form swaggered out of the barn. Her palms went damp. Her knees turned to gelatin. Only one man had ever had that effect on her—one wonderful man.

Hawk. Joy exploded through her at the mere sight of him shouldering out into the rain. She drank in the sight of his cherished face, his blue eyes. His stalwart, noble presence made her feel alive.

"Figured I would find you here." He jammed his fists into his pockets. He didn't look like a man who was glad to see her.

No, he wouldn't be, she reminded herself. *You broke his heart, remember? You hurt him to save yourself.* She wasn't proud of it, but she could see now that she was still letting fear rule her. She might as well be back in that mine shaft, trapped in a grave of fear and darkness. That was no way to live. She squared her shoulders, steeled her spine and tapped down the concrete walkway, splashing in his direction.

"Hawk, what brings you here?" She was pleased with how normal she sounded, not at all like a woman who had been battling regrets or another lost chance at love. She hiked her chin higher, digging deep for every scrap of courage. Facing him was like seeing the littered remains of another lost future, more impossible dreams. She was stronger than loss, tougher than sorrow.

"I came to say goodbye to Comanche." No hint of emotion on his face. No warmth in his words. No welcoming smile softening his granite face.

"Comanche?" Her footstep faltered, her knees went weaker. She froze in place on the walkway, halfway between Hawk and the barn. The wind swirled rain and stirred the grass near her feet and the trees lining the walkway moaned with the wind.

He hadn't come to see her at all, she realized. Disappointment turned to torture. She wanted to dart straight for the office door. After all, work was waiting. But she would not use an excuse to avoid him or anything, not any longer. She fisted her hands, determined to see this through the right way. "I hope you two had a good chat."

"He seemed glad to see me. I'm short three peppermints." Hawk did her the courtesy of not smiling—of not reminding her of the dimples she loved and the tiny crinkles that dug handsomely into the corners of his eyes.

Whatever she did, she refused to acknowledge the memories trying to flood her brain. She would not remember him offering her his heart. She would not remember riding horses with him, or standing in front of a Christmas tree's glow or how her hand fit perfectly within his. The one thing she could not do—that she could never do—was remember the bliss of his kiss, the gentleness, the sweetness. Or her strength would falter. He looked all warrior, not like a man who had come to hope for a second chance at love.

"Seems I'll be shipping out earlier than expected." He sounded impersonal, as if they had never been more than passing acquaintances. As if the last few weeks hadn't happened and she hadn't obliterated his feelings.

"But you were on leave."

"I'm probably going to cut it short."

"Probably?" Realization dawned across her face. "Oh, you've decided to head out."

"I haven't made it official yet, but that's my plan." He stopped, unable to bridge the rest of the distance between them. Raindrops danced on the concrete he could not make himself cross. "I'm just tying up loose ends. Saying goodbye to friends."

"I hope you have a good tour." The wind blew a shock of hair into her face and she brushed it back. "Just come back safe and sound."

"I'll do my best." Being here hurt him something fierce, but he had come to say something, and he wouldn't leave until the job was done. "How's the truck running?"

"As good as when it was brand-new."

"I'm glad. An afternoon's job well worth it." Seeing her forlorn and hurting was like a bullet to his chest. He didn't want to make this harder for her. If he put in his paperwork, then he had to head off to Afghanistan knowing there were no second chances. No maybes. That he wasn't destroying a remote chance with her because of it. He wanted more for his life, and he was not afraid to fight for it.

"Thank you for all you have done for me. I can't begin to tell you." She hesitated.

For a moment he thought he saw something change on her face, the quietest wish, the deepest longing for him. But then it was gone, and he couldn't be sure. Then he wasn't sure at all.

He was standing like an idiot in the rain, praying for a sign—any sign, the smallest sign—that he hadn't been wrong. That he hadn't mistaken friendship and gratitude for something grander. Everything within him wanted to ask her if there was a way they could make this work, if he had a chance of capturing her heart. But he could not do it yet. He could not risk frightening her away a second time. He had to tread carefully.

"It was nothing." He shrugged off her thanks for the few odds and ends he'd done. "A few nails here, an adjustment there, a new part to install. It was my pleasure."

"I wasn't talking about things. You helped *me*." She laid a hand over her heart. "I will never forget what you gave me."

At her words, everything went still. Even the rain seemed to stop falling. "What did I do?"

"You reminded me that there are precious gifts in this life and they are worth the cost."

For a moment—just a split second—he thought he saw a question in her beautiful brown eyes. A silent plea that settled in his soul. Hope resonated throughout his entire being. "How did I do that, sunshine?"

"I don't know. It's as if I came back to life the moment you first took my hand." She took a step closer. "I'm sorry for what I said. I hurt you, and I regret that more than you know. Please forgive me."

"Done. Don't worry about it. It's already forgotten." The shadows had slipped away from him, along with the tension of pain on his face. He stood straight and tall, invincible and every last bit of her only dream.

If he was anything less of a man, then she wouldn't be hurting like this. She wouldn't be falling apart over having lost him. She wouldn't be prepared to risk her heart again. But how did she tell him? She didn't have the words. All she had was emotion carrying her toward him. "I never wanted to see you again. I wanted to mean it, but you made me love again."

"I *made* you?"

"I couldn't stop myself." She fought to hold back her feelings. She told herself to be sensible. She couldn't afford to love him. He would go off on mission after mission, risking life and limb and her heart. She'd done it once and lost. Losing like that again would be too much. She knew the cost. She knew how much it would hurt. "I didn't want to love anyone again. I couldn't help loving you."

"You don't know how good that is to hear."

He closed his eyes briefly, as if giving thanks. When he opened them, she could read his devotion. "The moment I looked down into that mine and saw your precious face, I was a goner. I love you, September, with all I am and all I will ever be. I was miserable back home facing the dreams I'd lost."

"What dreams?"

"The ones with you at my side every step of the way. Starting family traditions, singing around the piano, family get-togethers and our wedding." He cleared his throat, as if overcome by emotion. "I stood up for my best man. I was happy for him. Don't get me wrong. I want him and Lexie to live happily ever after. But I want one of those, too. I want forever with you, September."

Forever. Panic lashed at her. If she wanted to start believing in fairy tales again and in the kind of love that remained true and everlasting, then she shouldn't fall in love with a Ranger. But her heart refused to listen.

"I need to know if you want that, too." Hawk's plea warmed the rain and chased the sting from the wind. "If there's any possibility, any at all. I have to know."

She was breaking apart, the reasons why she

couldn't love Hawk crumbling into dust. She had no shields left, no safeguards, no way to stop loving him. Love was a risk, for anyone, anytime. She knew the cost of loving a soldier. The endless worry. The sacrifice. The hardship. But was Hawk worth it?

The answer stood in front of her, a man of noble strength she could not live without. One word filled her mind, without doubt, without condition. "Yes."

"Yes?" Uncertainty turned to joy. His eyes twinkled, his grin flashed, dimples dug deep as instead of hugging her, which she expected, or doing something like punching his fist into the air, he went down on one knee. "Then I have another question for you. It's one I've been rehearsing most of the night, on the flight and during the drive here. September, will you marry me?"

"Marry you?" She went weak. The blood drained from her face. Her legs turned to rubber.

He rose, taking her into his arms, offering her the security of his chest and the shelter of his arms. His lips brushed her temple in light, tender kisses. Each one a silent promise, a promise no words could do justice to.

"I love you so much, Hawk." It was terrifying to think of opening her heart fully again, but a smart woman learned from the lessons in her life. "Yes. I would love to be your wife. On one condition."

"What? Name it."

"That we don't waste a moment of the time we have together." She adored Hawk. The power of her feelings terrified her, but she was certain of her choice. "No long engagements. No big wedding to plan. No putting off what we want to do."

"I like the sound of that." He pulled a ring from his pocket and cradled her left hand in his. The platinum band glided over her finger. The square-cut sapphire surrounded by diamonds glowed. "Maybe we can start planning on our next date."

"Date?" She felt full to the brim and overflowing with love and hope. She couldn't think what he was talking about. "You just said you were being deployed—"

"I'm dropping out of the Rangers for you."

"No, Hawk. I'm not asking you to give up the job you love."

"I love you more, sunshine." He brushed the damp hair away from her face, his touch affectionate and comforting. "You have been hurt enough. I don't want to put you through that again. I talked to my commanding officer and since you've agreed to marry me, I'm going to stay. I will be helping with training right here at Fort Lewis."

"And that would make you happy?"

"Happier than I can imagine. That's what I want to do for you, September. To live for you. I promise you this. I will do my best for you every day of my life. You are my light."

"And you are mine." Never had she felt so blessed. She had received the best Christmas gift—one of true, everlasting love. She was a girl who could believe in dreams again, because she was holding one in her arms. Her amazing husband-to-be drew her tightly against him and covered her mouth with his. Their kiss was triumphant. As if heaven thought so, too, the wind gusted and the rain turned to snow.

Epilogue

One year later

The lights of the Christmas tree blinked cheerfully in front of the big picture window. September Hawkins, with her arms wrapped around a gigantic bowl of popcorn, froze in the middle of the kitchen. Every once in a while it still hit her. The wonderful man sitting on her couch was her husband. They were looking forward to their first anniversary next month, and she still couldn't believe it was real. Her life was a dream come true.

"Hey, sunshine." Hawk looked up from his half-finished string of popcorn. "Good thing you've got a fresh batch there. My bowl is mysteriously empty."

"I wonder how that could have happened."

She was crossing the room without realizing it, drawn closer to him with a love that would never end. Bing Crosby was serenading them in the background, a pile of presents gleamed and glinted beneath the live Christmas tree and outside the window the lit stars were joined by a small family of lighted reindeer. "You eat everything that isn't nailed down."

"It's a fault of mine. Just add it to the list." Grinning, he set down his work and rose to help her. "You should not be carrying anything."

"As if the popcorn bowl is too heavy. Really. You are overprotective, Hawk." She didn't mind that when he took the bowl from her, he took the time to give her a kiss. His hand settled on her gently swollen midsection. "I'm fine. You are just using this as an excuse to come snuggle me."

"I'll use any excuse I can get." To prove it, he dispensed with the bowl and wrapped both arms around her. "We have to take advantage of the time we have left. Three more months and we won't be alone anymore."

"I can't wait to hold Little Timothy Frank Hawkins for the first time."

"Neither can I."

Happy, September wrapped her arms around

Hawk's neck. Hawk had kept his promise to her. His vow to make her happy. To live his life for her. Her world was one of light and love, of joy and fulfillment. What a beautiful year she'd had first as his fiancée, as his bride and then his wife. Soon, they would be starting a new chapter of their marriage together—parenthood. Already their nursery was taking shape. Good thing the town house had three bedrooms. It would accommodate them for several more years before they had to upsize. For now, this place was just right. Full of love, filled with happiness and hope.

To think she had almost missed this opportunity, this life. It was hard to believe now she had once been too afraid to love him. She would have missed out on the greatest year of her life. And the best, she knew, was yet to come.

"Mistletoe." Hawk's lips grazed her cheek. "I felt it was my duty and obligation to hang it up while you were making the popcorn. After all, we have to start our own traditions."

"Yes, we do," she agreed. "Traditions are very important."

His kiss was sweet perfection, as their every kiss had been and always would be.

Life is beautiful, she thought, grateful to God

for her blessings. The Lord's gentle grace had brought her through the darkness of her grief to this beautiful new beginning.

* * * * *

Dear Reader,

You may remember Hawk from *A Soldier for Keeps*. When I was writing that book, I fell in love with the tall, dark and silent soldier. I know he was searching for the Lord's leading, and I wondered if he had found his way. As I began writing Hawk's story, I fell even more in love with this faithful, solid, good-to-the-core man. I admire the choices he makes with his life and the tender way he falls in love with the heroine, September Stevens. September is a woman who is wrestling with grief, and who is struggling with her faith. I hope you are encouraged by her story, and that you enjoy watching how God leads September and Hawk to hope and everlasting love.

Thank you so much for choosing *The Soldier's Holiday Vow*.

Wishing you the best of blessings this Christmas season,

Jillian Hart

Questions for Discussion

1. At the beginning of the story, how would you describe September's character? What are her weaknesses and her strengths? How is the mine she's fallen into metaphoric?

2. What is September's reaction when she first sees Hawk? What does this tell you about her? How is Hawk characterized through her perspective?

3. In the beginning of the story, September feels as if loss has changed the woman she used to be. Have you ever felt that way? Explain.

4. What is behind Hawk's decision to bring September flowers, a pizza and his mission to help her out? What does this say about him?

5. Why is it painful for September to see Hawk? How does this change throughout the story? Why does it change?

6. Why does Hawk feel that he is too tough and too scarred for love? How do these feelings change?

7. How does September rebuild her faith? How does God lead her through her fears? Have you ever struggled with similar issues?

8. September believes that friendship is the only kind of love she can count on. How is this belief challenged through the book? How is God's leading evident?

9. What role does September's love for causes and fund-raising play in the story?

10. When does Hawk realize he is in love with September?

11. What do you think are the important themes? How do they relate to the Christmas season?

12. What do you like most about September and Hawk as a couple? How do you know they are meant for each other?

13. How would you describe September's faith journey? How are her and Hawk's faiths strengthened through the story?

14. September believes that if she opens her heart she will be too vulnerable, and that's too great of a risk to take. What changes her mind? What does she learn about love and life?

REQUEST YOUR FREE BOOKS!

2 FREE RIVETING INSPIRATIONAL NOVELS
PLUS 2 FREE MYSTERY GIFTS

Love Inspired®
SUSPENSE

REQUEST YOUR FREE BOOKS!

2 FREE INSPIRATIONAL NOVELS
PLUS 2
FREE
MYSTERY GIFTS

Love Inspired.
HISTORICAL
INSPIRATIONAL HISTORICAL ROMANCE

YES! Please send me 2 FREE Love Inspired® Historical novels and my 2 FREE mystery gifts (gifts are worth about $10). After receiving them, if I don't wish to receive any more books, I can return the shipping statement marked "cancel." If I don't cancel, I will receive 4 brand-new novels every month and be billed just $4.74 per book in the U.S. or $5.24 per book in Canada. That's a savings of at least 21% off the cover price. It's quite a bargain! Shipping and handling is just 50¢ per book in the U.S. and 75¢ per book in Canada.* I understand that accepting the 2 free books and gifts places me under no obligation to buy anything. I can always return a shipment and cancel at any time. Even if I never buy another book, the two free books and gifts are mine to keep forever.

102/302 IDN F5CY

Name _____ (PLEASE PRINT)

Address _____ Apt. #

City _____ State/Prov. _____ Zip/Postal Code

Signature (if under 18, a parent or guardian must sign)

Mail to the Harlequin® Reader Service:
IN U.S.A.: P.O. Box 1867, Buffalo, NY 14240-1867
IN CANADA: P.O. Box 609, Fort Erie, Ontario L2A 5X3

Want to try two free books from another series?
Call 1-800-873-8635 or visit www.ReaderService.com.

* Terms and prices subject to change without notice. Prices do not include applicable taxes. Sales tax applicable in N.Y. Canadian residents will be charged applicable taxes. Offer not valid in Quebec. This offer is limited to one order per household. Not valid for current subscribers to Love Inspired Historical books. All orders subject to credit approval. Credit or debit balances in a customer's account(s) may be offset by any other outstanding balance owed by or to the customer. Please allow 4 to 6 weeks for delivery. Offer available while quantities last.

Your Privacy—The Harlequin® Reader Service is committed to protecting your privacy. Our Privacy Policy is available online at www.ReaderService.com or upon request from the Harlequin Reader Service.

We make a portion of our mailing list available to reputable third parties that offer products we believe may interest you. If you prefer that we not exchange your name with third parties, or if you wish to clarify or modify your communication preferences, please visit us at www.ReaderService.com/consumerchoice or write to us at Harlequin Reader Service Preference Service, P.O. Box 9062, Buffalo, NY 14269. Include your complete name and address.

LIHDIR13R